Also by George Franklin

Non-fiction

"Raisin Bran and Other Cereal Wars"

"So You Think You Want to Run for Congress"

INCENTIVES
THE HOLY WATER OF FREE ENTERPRISE

Copyright © 2020 George Franklin
Cover Design and Art Direction: Julie Davis

Special thanks to the indefatigable Becky O'Dell who is a dear
colleague that makes it all happen.

FPA Books
Atlanta, GA

This book may be ordered through booksellers or by visiting
GeorgeFranklinAuthor.com

This novel is a work of fiction. The characters, names, incidents, dialogue
and plot are the products of the author's imagination or are used fictitiously.
Any resemblance to actual persons, companies or events
is purely coincidental.

ISBN: 978-1-7334444-2-2 (Paperback)
ISBN: 978-1-7334444-3-9 (e-Book)

Printed in the United States of America

GEORGE FRANKLIN

PURE UNADULTERATED FUN!

A NOVEL

In¢entives

The Holy Water of Free Enterprise

FPA BOOKS

In Memory
of
Rob Crabb

A straight shooter who always cautioned
the corporate higher-ups about those
"pesky bureaucrats."

ONE

E xplaining or apologizing for the weather was just part of the job, but it sure got tiresome. Hell, everywhere has one season when it is too hot, too cold or too something, but that reality was lost on most prospects who only seemed to care about the cold. Today would be no different.

Slate-gray sky, 17 degrees, slight wind from the northwest and a chance of flurries. Quite a place to try and recruit business, thought Red Johansson as he pushed the garage door opener button on his black 2018 Buick Regal. Only American metal would do in Michigan.

Red Johansson had been President of Battle Creek First, the economic development arm of the City of Battle Creek, for nine years. As the home of Kellogg Company, it was the self-proclaimed cereal capital of the world and so promoted by that pitiful sign on I-94. Not much to work with, but at least it was the capital of something.

He was off this morning to meet another prospect at the W.K. Kellogg Airport, which usually entails a plane load of pompous corporate types all vying to be the most obsequious to whoever was the ranking company officer on board. They, in turn, would prove their mettle by being obnoxious, difficult and generally rude to the economic development official who had come to meet them, in this case, Red.

Part of girding his loins for this type of arrival was a stop at his favorite coffee shop, the Brownstone, for a shot of java. He liked the Brownstone because it was real, not like the phony Starbucks with made-up corporate names for large, medium and small. His whole professional life was putting up with corporate BS. So why start the day with it?

"Hey, Red, you are here early for a Monday. Prospects coming in?" bellowed Chuck, the always upbeat owner of the Brownstone as Red stomped the snow off his feet by the door.

How in the world does this guy stay so positive, much less make a living doing this, mulled Red before answering. "Yes, some oil guys are coming in looking for fracking sites over on the lakeshore. Guess we are going to become the new North Dakota. Might as well since it is fricking liquid gold."

"Better be careful with that, cautioned Chuck. The eco-terrorists are going bat shit over that issue, and it has become the cause célèbre and a big fundraiser for them. They have the Hollywood types and other crazed liberals all jumped up about it even though they really don't have a clue what they are talking about. I must admit it does make me a little nervous not knowing what it could do to our water supply. Look at those poor bastards in Flint. We don't need another one of those."

"Don't worry, Chuck," retorted Red. "There have been hundreds of studies commissioned by the American Petroleum Institute, all of which confirm fracking does no harm, and one even says it causes hummingbirds to become bigger and more numerous. How can anybody be against that?"

"I don't know, Red, but just go slow with this one," warned Chuck.

"Okay, okay, I get it. Now how about my usual large, and jack it up with an extra shot of caffeine. I think I am going to need it with this group."

Red Johansson put on a good front, but the reality was he was beginning to hate his job and the corporate boot lickers he had to deal with. He and his wife, Ingrid, had moved to Battle Creek after attending St. Olaf College in Minnesota, where they had met as the only two white students majoring in African American studies. They had hoped to open an Afro Sheen Hair Franchise in the College's Swedish Cultural Center to cater to the six members of an African American student body but for some reason could not get the support of the administration of St. Olaf. Red then decided to join the family restaurant business, which was an "all you can eat Swedish buffet" located across the street from the Minnesota Viking's football team training camp. Perplexing as it was, costs always seemed to exceed revenue, and the restaurant went bust. Another in a series of financial failures by his father, who had poignantly named his son "Red" after exclaiming at his birth, "This will really put me further in the red."

The business world had not been good to him. He was adrift but still self-confident. He was a natural salesman, having been told for years he could "talk a dog off a meat wagon." All he needed was an opportunity. Plus, maybe a dog and a meat wagon.

Finally, it came to him late one night watching world wrestling on cable TV. An infomercial for a correspond-ence course in the fast-growing and exciting career field of economic development. The course only required an up-front payment of $500, which fully qualified for the federal student loan program and could be paid back over 25 years. The course itself was taught by "expert instructors and practitioners in the field" and "guaranteed you a certif-icate of completion" within two weeks, after which you would be ready to enter the "fast-paced life of an economic developer." The commercial ended with the one-time student driving off into the sunset in a Corvette convertible with a Dolly Parton look-a-like in the passenger seat.

"Ingrid, this is it," screamed Red to his wife, who was upstairs watching reruns of Dr. Phil. "Let me have your Visa card — mine is maxed out — so I can get in on the special TV promotion by calling within the next five minutes. This is a moment that can change our lives."

"Oh my God," exclaimed Ingrid. "The last course you signed up for in Logistics Transportation and Mass Distribution resulted in a part-time job driving a Good Humor truck in Minneapolis the two weeks before Christmas. Why is this going to be any different?"

"Listen, Ingrid, you have to have faith in me. This course will open up a whole new career. It will expose me to the captains of industry, the movers and shakers of the free enterprise system. It will teach me how our capitalist system really works."

"And how will it do that?" asked Ingrid.

"It tells you how to get money from the government."

"Oh shit, here we go again. Take my Visa."

"I love ya, sweetheart." Red dialed 1-800-YES-FREE.

TWO

Bogey Jackson and Skeeter Williams were losers in every sense of the word. A genealogical trait not hard to understand, considering their family lineage. Born and raised in the little town of Hahira, Georgia — whose claim to fame is the annual Honey Bee Festival — they both came from families who brought to mind the movie *Deliverance.*

Bogey's father was euphemistically referred to as "a traveling man," which in South Georgia parlance meant no one, including his mother, knew who is father was. His mother, albeit employed, had capped her career as a pricing manager at the Dollar General. Skeeter likewise had a sketchy upbringing. His father, who "was given to the cups" would routinely in the evening over a bottle of Ten High Bourbon serenade his wife, Betty Lou, on his ukulele with a rendition of his favorite country song, "You're the Reason Our Kids Are So Ugly." Sometimes for the sake of variety, he would belt out his version of "I Wouldn't Take Her to a Dog Fight Because I'm Afraid She'd Win." Betty

Lou, on the other hand, would spend most her evenings working on her newsletter for the Daughters of the Confederacy, which was sponsored by a local restaurant whose advertising slogan was "Eat like Paula Deen — you ain't fat, you're healthy."

Bogey and Skeeter never had a chance. They were little men with little minds, but you had to give them credit for trying. Sadly, all they had to show for their efforts after 22 years on this earth were unemployment checks, food stamps, a couple of Trump Make America Great Again baseball caps and a 1984 Ford F-150 pickup truck with a bumper sticker that proclaimed "If I had to lead my life over, I would lead it over a liquor store."

How they had gotten to this forlorn juncture in life was painfully evident to everyone in Hahira. They weren't very bright.

The first glimpse of their lack of entrepreneurial acumen appeared when they were in their late teens and Skeeter persuaded his 84-year-old grandmother to invest her life savings in an outdoor country music venue he and Bogey planned to launch in an abandoned Little League park. Opening night looked like it was going to be a smashing success. Ticket sales were brisk after they announced the opening act would be the nationally renowned band with the hit single "Mama Get a Hammer (There's a Fly on Papa's Head)." First-class entertainment with the promise of unlimited fine spirits and gourmet food for an all-inclusive price created an aura of a beautiful evening under the stars. As the flyers proudly beckoned: "Come be part of the new Nashville of the South."

That first evening, over 300 eager patrons began to arrive as the sun was setting, a sea of pickup trucks and Confederate flags not seen since that time the country fair announced free elephant ears for every member of the National Rifle Association. It looked like a perfect evening, but trouble was brewing. The band was a no-show and was quickly replaced by a tuba player from the neighboring Hephzibah High School marching band. The fine spirits consisted of warm Bud Light, and the gourmet food was cold pigs in a blanket from Walmart. What really was the undoing of the night, however, was the gnats. You see, Hahira is located below what in Georgia is infamously called the gnat line. An area where on every summer evening, millions of biting gnats descend on any human being out and about. They bite and swarm, and no amount of slapping or waving will ward them off, and on that night they descended with a vengeance. The crowd turned on each other as slaps turned into hits, which turned into fights. Bogey, intending to calm the crowd, attempted to sell used funeral home fans for $5 and bug spray for $10 to make a few extra bucks, but this only exacerbated the situation, turning the patrons into an unruly mob who stormed his vending booth. Finally, in a fit of collective rage, almost 250 incensed patrons marched from the ballpark to Skeeter's grandmother's assisted living home demanding a refund. His grandmother managed to escape on her motorized wheelchair but not until significant damage had already been done to the creeper home (so called by the number of residents creeping about with their walkers) welcome room. Not to mention the front yard, which had been torn to shreds by pickups doing doughnuts.

There is a lot of nowhere around Hahira, and Bogey and Skeeter knew every inch of it as they mindlessly cruised the back roads in their dilapidated F-150.

"Did you not know that in 2013 there were 2,768 craft breweries in the United States?" blurted out Bogey on one of their innumerable vacuous meanderings.

"What the fuck does that have to do with anything?" cracked Skeeter while snuffing out his cigarette in the almost empty Bud Light can.

Bogey went on, "Well, you and I have a proud heritage of alcohol consumption and distribution dating back to prohibition. Both of our great grandfathers did time for bootlegging, and our DUI records attest to our affinity for a beer now and then. Hell, even your limited love life with Pattie Sue was made possible by her copious consumption of vodka mixed with Mountain Dew."

"Okay, maybe the vodka did have something to do with her suggesting we run off and get married in Myrtle Beach that night, but I really thought she loved me until she left with the semi driver at closing time," lamented Skeeter.

"Listen, Skeeter, alcohol is in our veins, literally and figuratively. It is part of our DNA and, as such, it's a calling we need to pursue. Booze is a multi-billion-dollar industry where opportunity abounds."

"And just how the hell do we do that? Two guys, dead broke, with no skills. Sure, we know how to drink it, but we don't know how to make it or even sell it, legally anyways."

"I think I know. While in the waiting room at Earl's Tire Repair, I saw an article in the *National Enquirer* talking about how the government will give you money for job training for a vocation in new and developing fields in which you can demonstrate experience, interest and potential. Hell, with five DUIs between us, we clearly have the experience and interest, and all we have to do is convince them we have potential when we apply for the money."

Skeeter pulled out another cigarette from his T-shirt pocket, lit it and took a drag as he popped another Bud Light, and with all the wherewithal he could muster with his alcohol addled brain responded, "You're full of shit."

THREE

G rowing up Cuban in Tampa meant, by definition being Catholic. Jesuit High School for the boys and the Academy of the Holy Names for the girls. Places you sent your children so they could learn discipline, integrity, and morals and where values were instilled on a daily basis. Not so with Armando Salazar and Rosa Castellano, two genetic miscreants who deserved each other.

Armando grew up in West Tampa, where he was noted for nothing. Skinny, medium height, greasy black hair and brown eyes and constantly wearing a "Tony" T-shirt, he was nondescript as imaginable in a neighborhood where everyone had names like Martinez, Gutierrez or Rodriguez. He was admitted to Jesuit solely on the basis of his mother, who was an indefatigable volunteer for every undertaking or committee Father Rapacious, the Prefect of Discipline, would devise. His mom was hell bent that Armando would go to Jesuit and graduate. So much so that she made a daily devotional to St. Jude, patron saint of the impossible, that Armando would actually become something. Possibly too difficult a task even for the saint of impossible.

Rosa, an only child of a fifth-generation cigar family grew up in affluence in the Ybor City section of Tampa, where Cuban immigrants and the cigar business had settled. Her father, Ralph, was a ne'er-do-well, having inherited the family business, Castellano Cigars, from his father. Her mother, Cachita, was a socialite who took herself seriously, although no one else did. A former cosmetologist, she had zeroed in on Ralph as her ticket to the good life the moment they first met, when he groped her as a drunken pirate in the Gasparilla Parade — the Tampa version of Mardi Gras. Realizing the potential of the encounter, she shoved her business card for Cachita's House of Dreams down his pants, where he found it the next day. Thereafter, using her God-given talents, the rest was history.

The life of Cachita and Ralph was a social whirl, which left little time for Rosa. A shy, meek girl, she spent most of her time in her room listening to Gloria Estefan and Ricky Martin CDs, which should have been of concern to her parents, but isn't that why they sent her to the academy? The nuns assured them that this was just a phase and that the sweet smoke always emanating from her room was probably just incense, like the kind used at Mass, which connoted a spiritual side to her that would soon blossom.

Armando and Rosa became an "item" after meeting at a Youth for Christ rally, and they were made for each other. Two words for this twosome — average and boring. Average looks, average grades, average talent. If there was an award for the most mediocre, they would both win hands down. There was, however, one area in which they excelled — drugs. They were constantly stoned. Marijuana was their passion and area of expertise. Armando had even secured a pilot's license so that he could ferry high-grade Columbian from the Bahamas to Peter O. Knight Airport on Davis Islands in Tampa. His blandness was an asset since no one would suspect that anyone as boring and non-descript as he was would be a major mule in the drug trade.

Rosa was an equal partner in the drug distribution business with Armando and dubbed herself a consumer affairs specialist in charge of product preparation. She would meet him each night he arrived with a new shipment and unload the bales into a "borrowed" van from Castellano's Cigars, which she would drive to the cigar factory in Ybor City, back up to the loading dock, where Hector, a street person, would for a couple of bottles of Boone's Farm Apple Wine help her unload. All of this while the night guard was asleep or preoccupied looking at foldouts from *Latin Ladies Magazine.* Once inside, she would avail herself to the cigar rolling equipment to make massive joints that became known on the street as El Grandes. They were an instant hit demanding a premium price at high schools and colleges throughout the bay area.

Unbeknownst to her, the surreptitious appropriation of the cigar making equipment was having a beneficial impact on the Castellano Company. Turns out each time that Rosa made a new batch of El Grandes, the residue would become part of that week's cigar production, giving them a distinct taste and aroma, not to mention impact. Sales boomed. They became known as "Happy Smokes," which, for some strange reason, induced customers to have the munchies for deviled crabs, available through numerous food carts in and around Ybor City. An economic catalyst resulting in the Castellano Company being awarded the Community Partnership Award by the local Cuban American Club.

FOUR

J aap VanValkenberg and his wife, Berdenna, were
committed and dedicated adherents to the tenets of the
Dutch Reformed Church. A life filled with religion, family
and public service. Graduates of Calvin College in West
Michigan, a school dedicated to preparing students to
answer God's call and serve as his agents for salvation in
the world, they took their mission and responsibilities
quite seriously.

Public service had always been at the core of Jaap's
existence. Before graduating from Calvin, he had been
active in the Young Republicans College Chapter and
had organized a branch of the Moral Majority based on
the teachings of televangelist Jimmy Swaggart. When
Swaggart was defrocked as a result of sexual scandals with
prostitutes, he adroitly pivoted the organization to become
a chapter of Ernest Angley Ministries after watching the
Reverend Angley remove evil spirits on his weekly late
night television show. Jaap's press release announcing the
switch to the Angley organization extolled the ability of

the Reverend Angley to remove any evil spirits left by Reverend Swaggart by the laying on of hands. It was a seamless transition, and the number of dues-paying members increased.

In his senior year, Jaap attended a job fair at the college, where he spotted a booth for the Amway Corporation manned by two recruiters who resembled Mormons on a mission. They were, in fact, on a mission since they called themselves Ministers of Free Enterprise and were looking for "ambassadors" who would spread the word that "capitalism, profit and lower taxes" "would ameliorate if not resolve the social ills confronting the country and the world," while also making you rich selling soap. Perfect fit, thought Jaap — cleanliness next to Godliness. He would go door-to-door selling the product and make money, all the while developing a network of would-be supporters when he made that first run for elective office. His opportunity to serve in the public sector came sooner than expected. The incumbent, long-term State Senator Dirk Vanderveen, was secretly filmed on a beach in Aruba with a voluptuous 28-year-old female "lobbyist" for the distilled spirits industry; at the same time, his office had announced he was going to be attending a "religious retreat for personal spiritual revitalization." Despite his claims that the young woman was his niece and that the film was a smear attempt by the liberal media, he was forced to resign after his wife filed for divorce alleging "adultery, abandonment and mendacity."

Jaap, being a man of faith, immediately jumped into the breach. He held a press conference with Berdenna at his side to pray for the fallen senator.

"We must first concern ourselves with the spiritual well-being of Senator Vanderveen. Our God is a forgiving God, and we must adhere to that spirit, but let there be no misunderstanding that it is with great reluctance I am running. Duty calls."

Berdenna, with tears streaming down her cheeks, echoed his concerns, "We must think of his family first, and as we all know, none of us really knows what goes on in situations like this, but, oh, the pain his wife must feel." All the while wearing a Family First T-shirt as she wailed and sobbed uncontrollably while the TV cameras whirred.

Senator Vanderveen was toast.

Although the state capitol in Lansing was under total control of the Republicans, his own party, Jaap's campaign slogan, "Never have so few stolen so much," resonated with the people. He ran as an outsider, a maverick, not beholden to anyone. Six-figure donations he received from car dealers, beer wholesalers, chambers of commerce and gun lobbyists could easily be explained as simply recognition of his "independent thinking and faith in the free enterprise system." He easily defeated Senator Vanderveen in the primary election, and with an overwhelming Republican District, stomped his Democrat opponent, an ornithologist named Dr. Alfred Meek, in the general election. Off to Lansing.

Now in his second and last term, due to term limits, Jaap had begun to become concerned about what he would do after leaving the legislature. Other than those six months right after college as an Amway salesman, he had never had a real job. His seven years as a senator had been devoid of anything significant. In fact, he had only introduced two bills — both of which he had "borrowed" from other state legislators while attending the American Legislative Exchange Council (ALEC) meeting in Miami Beach. The first legislative proposal attempted to protect the civil rights of fat Caucasian people. An Indiana state representative attempting to block civil rights protections for gays and lesbians had, in Jaap's mind, cogently argued that since homosexuality was a "behavioral thing," just like overeating, they were all worthy of equal protection. His only other piece of legislation was based on an initiative by a New York legislator to create a "National Political Corruption Hall of Fame." Jaap was indignant that New York would try and corner the market on what would clearly be a major tourist attraction with an endless supply of new material to keep it current. "Failure to enact this legislation will abdicate an entire field of endeavor where Michigan has and continues to maintain a leadership role," his accompanying press release pronounced.

Neither bill ever made it out of committee.

Berdenna loved being the senator's wife. Born into a rural family, her father was a blueberry farmer, and her mother was a waitress at the Hawk's Nest Café. She was ambitious and dreamed of becoming "somebody." Her ambition, however, was limited by the fact that she had few distinguishing characteristics. Typical Dutch blonde hair, blue eyes and a Rubenesque corn queen figure. A good, but not great, student, no particular interest or avocation, nice girl, nice personality. Generally, Midwest and pleasant.

None of the ingredients for success and glamour, with one glaring exception — she had huge boobs. Two melons that would bowl guys over. Two attributes that had propelled her to teenage fame as the youngest winner of the Miss Asparagus Contest. Only 13 when she won this coveted title, she thanked the Lord Jesus Christ with "endowing her with his bounty." It was during her freshman year at Calvin that she began to realize what head turners they were, causing a young Jaap VanValkenberg to suffer whiplash when he first met her when they were entering a seminar on the Bible and pornography. Soon the couple fell into a deep rapture of Christian love, and Jaap on bended knee asked her to marry him on the video cam at half time of the epic battle of Dutchmen when Calvin College played Hope College in basketball.

FIVE

Boone Cartwright relished the well-deserved moniker "Dirtiest Man Alive," so deemed by the American Petroleum Institute when he was selected Wildcat Man of the Year.

"Those who see pollution as a problem don't understand the creation of wealth" was his usual refrain to those who criticized his oil drilling zest. "What the hell is a couple of dead fish when all this money can be made," he would advise his employees while goading them to drill farther and deeper. "The dirtier we get, the richer we get," was the company mantra.

Boone had made lots of money in the oil business, so much so that even though he was on his fourth wife, with three $100 million-plus divorces behind him, he was still in the billionaire class with all the trimmings. He had been brought up in a strict west Texas evangelical household where the family creed was "an eye for an eye, a tooth for a tooth and each man for himself." His father, Rod, had lived the creed and in doing so had made a fortune as a slumlord for migrant workers. The business model was as simple as it was ingenious. He would acquire second-hand trailers with loans from the Rural Economic Development fund of the U.S. Department of Agriculture using a front group he created called The Coalition for Economic Justice for the People. It was a coalition of one — Rod — ostensibly dedicated to "providing a multicultural, multi-lingual, diverse community dedicated to agricultural advancement." Simply put, it was a trailer park for illegal migrant workers, which also provided rental loans at usurious rates, assuring few complaints from fear of being deported while creating a hefty balance sheet.

Boone always credited his father with instilling in him an appreciation for the free market and an inherent distrust of the government. "Son," Rod would intone, "no sooner than the government lends you the money, you find out it comes with all sorts of strings attached attempting to justify the low rates. Why, they even want reports on how it is being used to advance the common good. Totally unreasonable demands imposed by feckless bureaucrats who clearly don't understand the free enterprise system. If Ronald Reagan were alive today, he would make sure that crony capitalism was allowed to flourish unencumbered by too much red tape."

Young Boone took his father's words to heart. After flunking out of Baylor (aka the Notre Dame of Baptists) his father made a large donation to the incumbent con-gressman, which opened a slot for Boone in the National

Guard, allowing him to avoid all that messy business in Southeast Asia. After 18 months as a "weekend warrior," he successfully petitioned for an early discharge citing "family and civic responsibilities." He was now free to pursue a career based on his faith in unbridled capitalism requiring a modicum of what he liked to refer to as "right-thinking government."

The opportunity he had been looking for presented itself when he saw a cadre of unemployed, dejected oil workers lined up at the unemployment office. He thought to himself, "Through hard work and my inheritance, I should be able to do something with those wells that have run dry and they have left behind. What if I were to purchase them through the Texas Abandoned Property Program, claim them as a "renewable resource" by using a toxic chemical solvent to loosen oil residue, which I can then sell to Jiffy Lube as part of their Environmental Awareness Initiative." Sure, the amount of oil retrieved would be de minimis and the profits even less so, but the real wealth was to be found in the tax code. You see, Boone had inherited hundreds of millions of dollars that had to be protected from Uncle Sam. By resurrecting these wells, he opened his fortune to the wondrous world of the tax code and specifically the lucrative windfall of the oil depletion allowance. Sure, there were some environmental issues with the runoff of the chemical solvent, but that was the price to be paid for progress. He had created an entire new world of opportunity called tax fracking.

SIX

B everly Hills, on the south side of Chicago, is an Irish Catholic enclave about as far away from its more famous cousin, Beverly Hills, California, as you can get. Surrounded by the kick-ass "Bad, Bad Leroy Brown" sections of the city, it is an insular environment controlled by priests, nuns, brothers and political patronage. Blacks and whites rarely mixed except for the occasional encounter on the football field, baseball diamond or basketball court. You grew up there going to St. Barnabas for grammar school and then for high school either to Brother Rice for the boys or Mother McCauley for the girls. Possibly attend some college with a compass heading in the name and then return, get married and start the process all over again. The place was one big cul-de-sac.

Sean O'Malley and Paddy Fitzpatrick epitomized the circular dead end of Beverly Hills. Their mothers had disdain for the medical admonition not to drink while pregnant, both claiming, "Hell, if drinking harmed the child, the Irish would be a race of mutants." Whether their mother's taste for the drink had anything to do with Sean and Paddy's slothful behavior will never be known. Neither scored very high on the IQ scale. Paddy, for instance, thought it intellectually stimulating to repeatedly ask Sister Cavanaugh during Catechism class, "If God is all powerful, can he make a rock so big he can't pick it up?" The class would immediately break out in guffaws, whereupon Sister Cavanaugh, ruler in hand, would beat him about the head while screaming, "Mr. Fitzpatrick, the answer is a matter of faith." About this time, Sean would blurt out in a stage whisper, "Well, if it is always just a matter of faith, why doesn't Notre Dame win every weekend!" For some reason his beating was always worse than the one Paddy would get.

The two young Irish Americans were inseparable, and upon barely graduating from Brother Rice decided jointly to attend a small liberal-arts Catholic college in suburban Chicago called Saint Procopius. The choice of this institution was made based on two key criteria; first, it was the only place that let them in; second, it was not known for its academic rigor. This latter aspect was confirmed in their minds on their first visit to the campus. Unbeknownst to them, the college was situated next to the state mental hospital, which had benches dotting the grounds. Pulling up to the facility, which they thought was the college, they spied two patients, pants unzipped, drooling while lounging on the bench, causing Sean to remark, "These guys don't look too sharp. I think we are going to do okay here."

"Agree," responded Paddy. "This is the kind of place we have been looking for."

Once enrolled, picking a major was their first big decision. Sean had been advised by his bartender cousin that figuring out which were the cupcake courses was easy. Just figure out what the jocks were taking and follow their lead. Plus, if you befriended a couple of football or basketball players, you could get access to their study, sheets which usually included the exam in advance.

No question it was going to be criminal justice or political science. Every member of the football team, except the kicker, was enrolled in one of these two majors and the same for the entire basketball team, absent the manager. Decision time resulted in a rare departure from the norm in that Sean and Paddy went their separate ways. Sean decided criminal justice was his ticket to a college degree, and Paddy went with political science.

Considering their backgrounds from Chicago, where crime and politics interconnect seamlessly, these were two areas of study for which they should have a knack. The two disciplines were part of their heritage. The ability to blur the line between corruption and good government was a trait imbued at an early age. They were taught in their youth that kickbacks to the local alderman were just part of the process to make government run more efficiently. The civics version of tithing! It didn't matter that neither Sean nor Paddy had a clue what in the real world they would do with these degrees. They were in college, their parents were still sending them money, and there was a bar named, as there is in every college town, The Library, with two-for-one drinks every night between 5 and 7.

SEVEN

R ed had done this drill of meeting corporate prospects innumerable times, but something about this crowd piqued his interest. Never before had oil interests come kicking the tires in Southwest Michigan — an area known more for blueberries than black gold.

Environmental Renewable Resources, LLC (ERR) proudly pronounced on its website that its founder and CEO, Boone Cartwright, had created the company "to take the resources God has given us, reallocate them using the energy of the divine and in so doing revive, resurrect and complete the metaphysical life of our communities." Red wasn't really sure what to make of all that, but whatever it meant, it sure sounded good.

The initial call to Battle Creek first had come from a Ms. Brooke Blackstone, who had introduced herself as confidential assistant to Mr. Cartwright, founder and CEO of ERR.

The company, she explained, was interested in touring some abandoned oil-drilling sites in the town of Glenn, about an hour and a half drive from Battle Creek on the Lake Michigan shore. Confidentiality was a must considering the highly competitive nature of the oil business, but the economic rewards to the area would be significant if successful. "Usually an endeavor such as we anticipate would require a hundred or so new employees, and as a company, we are committed to a multicultural and ethnic work force drawing from the Native American, African American, Irish American, Latin American, Latvian American and other culturally deprived communities in the area." Brooke went on to explain that given the scope of the investment contemplated a "logistical, technical, transportation and research center may be required and would be headquartered in Battle Creek." She concluded her introduction by emphasizing that "ERR was a self-reliant organization fostered by its western roots where competitive capitalism was the coin of the realm. On second thought, however, and as part of due diligence are there any federal, state or local incentives that might be available?"

Red could see the sleek Falcon 900 jet on final approach to the W.K. Kellogg Airport as he approached from Dickman Road in the black Cadillac Escalade he had rented for the day. A little nervous as he was unprepared to discuss incentives since, to be honest, he wasn't sure what ERR really did. This uncertainty had not prevented him from briefing the Battle Creek First Board on the arrival of a "game changing" prospect he had "assiduously courted for over two years" that would be a "catalyst for an economic renaissance for all of Southwest Michigan." So what if none of that was true. His performance review was coming up, and that was about all he had to show for it.

Short on substance, he was prepared to laud his visitors with personal flattery — an aspect of recruitment he found most valuable. Doing your homework on who you were dealing with and how to make them shine in front of the boss was his strong suit. There were to be three others in addition to Boone, and Red had the rundown on each.

Brooke, the confidential assistant, had an unusual but meteoric corporate career. Mr. Cartwright had first spotted her from the owner's box of the Dallas Cowboys, where he was a guest with his third wife, and Brooke was lead cheerleader on the 40-yard line. Claiming he always had a good eye for talent, Boone asked the team's Director of Development and Community Affairs if he could arrange for him to interview her the next day at The Gentlemen's Lounge, just a few blocks from his corporate office. Suffice it to say, they hit it off. The 26-year-old curvaceous cheerleader with Texas big blonde hair came suitably attired in a mini skirt, four-inch heels and a plunging neckline that revealed between her size 40 breasts a tattoo of a nuclear mushroom cloud inscribed "The Promised Land." Forgoing the formal questionnaire provided by the Human Resources Department of ERR after she assured him she was quite capable of taking confidential dictation, he downed his third martini and offered her the position of chief happiness officer. He went on to explain that as a corporate officer, she would report directly to him and that she would be entitled to a company paid apartment next to his auxiliary office. Her duties would include being available evenings and some early mornings in what he called "flex time," but she would be compensated quite well and evaluated on her ability to make him happy. As far as Red could determine, she was extremely successful at her corporate duties.

Also on the plane was Montavious Sharp, the Vice President of Purpose, Outreach, Diversity and Inclusion, a multi-faceted position that drew heavily on his experience and education. Montavious had grown up in the fashionable Buckhead neighborhood of Atlanta. His father was a noted physician who consulted with the Centers for Disease Control (CDC), and his mother was a partner with one of the major law firms. He attended historically black Alcorn State University, majoring in self-awareness but soon found that program boring and uninspiring and decided to focus on issues of political oppression, financial subjugation and class warfare. As an extension of this newfound consciousness, he founded a chapter of the National Indigenous Peoples Movement and appointed himself Comrade in Chief. Although an African American and not indigenous, he argued he qualified as a "trans-ethnic" just as the white woman who had become president of a local chapter of the NAACP qualified as "transracial." Montavious believed that the "trans-movement" was bigger than typical racial stereotypes. This positioning so flummoxed the university administration that it decided to appoint Montavious as Chair of the Student Commission to Review and Rewrite History. The commission was to be guided by a belief contained in the student body motto, "The cards you play are based on the cards you are dealt, but if you don't like them, then just demand a new hand."

Boone heard about Montavious through his mother's law firm, which had been retained to defend ERR LLC in a lawsuit charging it with "wholesale, rampant racial and sexual discrimination." Realizing he was in damage control mode, Boone was in need of a front man experienced in manipulation and obfuscation. Enter Montavious. Boone knew this was his man from the first interview.

When asked about his grade point, Montavious countered that grades "were merely a continuation of bourgeois subjugation." Questioned about his being busted twice for smoking crack, he lashed back that drugs were a "therapeutic reaction to the stress of being a social activist and a full-time student, the context of which demands an apology from the university and its callous, indifferent Gestapo jackbooted enforcers." Boone was completely bewildered and befuddled by these answers and knew right away Montavious was a perfect fit.

The final member of the entourage was the Director of Real Estate, Ron White. A complete corporate drone with a white, pasty complexion, mousy brown hair, a gaunt physique and an uncanny spineless ability to agree with everything his boss said. Clearly, he was someone who had never read *Profiles in Courage* by John F. Kennedy. He had two critical roles to play in every new business venture. First, agree with everything Boone said. Second, be the front man to pull the rug out when it became time to renege on whatever commitments, promises or assurances ERR LLC had made to economic development authorities or government officials. He was the complete corporate man of mendacity.

"Hi, Sam. It's me, Red. Got a plane coming in. Will you open the gate?" he shouted after pushing the call button on the electronic gate to the entrance to the general aviation hanger at W.K. Kellogg Airport. Gradually, the gate swung open and Red drove out to the tarmac so he would be at the bottom of the steps when the jet arrived.

Sure enough, right on time, taxing forth was a green and gold Falcon 900 with call letters BC 001 (BC for Boone Cartwright, and green and gold, the school colors of Baylor where a waste disposal system had been named in his honor). As is always the case, the first one down the steps is one of the pilots in uniform who states the obvious to Red, shivering while trying to appear not to be cold.

"Hi, I am Bill Jackson. We are from ERR LLC. Mr. Cartwright and others will be down momentarily."

"Welcome to Battle Creek," responded Red, "We have been looking forward to your visit."

It would be a few minutes before anyone would descend. Protocol of the power dance dictates that the corporate types make the economic development reps wait. Finally, the curtain opens and Boone bounds down the steps dressed in the perfunctory cowboy hat, bolo tie with a Baylor emblem as the centerpiece and a fur coat that looked like it was a converted animal rug. Next came Brooke, sidestepping so her six-inch heels didn't get caught, draped in an American lynx fur coat, followed by Montavious who looked as if he had won the Mr. Burberry Award, and finally Ron with scruffy brown shoes wearing a "two for one" Joseph Banks suit and, in an attempt to look officious, touting a weathered briefcase.

"Hello, there, young fellow. I'm Boone Cartwright, this is Brooke Blackstone, our Chief Happiness Officer, Montavious Sharp, our Vice President of Product, Outreach, Diversity and Inclusion and Ron White, who does our real estate stuff."

"Welcome, everyone to Battle Creek, and don't let the weather deter you — it is an aberration. Our mean temperature this time of year is 72.5° as a result of the warm winds off Lake Michigan we call the Caribbean affect," responded Red.

"Never heard of such," exclaimed Brooke in a Texas drawl.

"Okay, everyone, in the car," directed Red. "The drive to Glenn is just a little over an hour. Ron, why don't you sit up front with me. Mr. Cartwright, Brooke and Montavious you are in the back where I have some fresh coffee. We can discuss your visit on the ride over so I can better understand your business and exactly what your interests and needs might be. Also, feel free to ask me any questions about the region or the lake shore."

"What lake?" queried Brooke.

"Why, Lake Michigan, of course," answered Red incredulously.

"I thought we were going to Battle Creek, Nebraska. I have already done extensive research on the operations of a unicameral legislature," exclaimed Brooke. There was silence for a while as they drove down I-94 west and then north on Highway 131. Finally heading west again on state road 43.

It was Montavious who finally broke the stillness. "Red, if we were to make an investment in Glenn and employ local members of the Chippewa and Huron tribes, might some workforce training dollars be available from the state?"

"I'm sure they would be," replied Red. Members of the legislature are always sensitive to the needs of Native Americans — you're not interested in a casino are you?"

"No, our interest is in identifying sites that abound with natural resources, where we can restore the area to its original God-given bounty while providing the local community a sense of pride and worth by creating a vibrant local economy with high-paying jobs."

"I thought we were looking for an old oil well," chimed in Brooke. Silence again.

Finally, Red broke in, "Glenn is the perfect place for you."

EIGHT

They were dim bulbs, but not totally lacking in ambition. Bogey was not afraid to attempt things for which he was totally unqualified, and Skeeter would readily follow. What and where to attempt their next failed endeavor kept their spirits and hopes alive.

Sure enough, eureka! One-day sitting in the food stamp office flipping through a three-year-old edition of *Field & Stream,* Bogey eyed an ad for "Adventure Seekers" interested in an opportunity in West Michigan. The ad, paid for with state funds under the Pure Michigan campaign, touted the interplay between charter fishing on Lake Michigan and the craft brew industry stretching from New Buffalo in the south all the way to Pentwater in the north. The enticing ad recited the "mutually compatible demographics" of those who fish and drink craft beer and how a "focused, directed marketing program" was an "unparalleled opportunity for outdoorsmen with a familiarity of grain-based products" to enter into a new dynamic field. Some "sales skills" were required, but job training funds were available. Simply call the Michigan State Office of the Unemployable, 1-800-MIS-FITS, for details and get ready for an exciting career.

This was too good to be true, thought Bogey, a job that combined their love of beer and the outdoors. Why, even Skeeter's experience as a route man for Critter Control might come in handy. Although the details of the job were somewhat sketchy, it was actually more nuanced than he would anticipate. The actual joint marketing program between the craft brewers and the charter fishermen had been developed in a collaborative undertaking by their respective trade associations — The Michigan Charter Fishermen League and the Michigan Craft Brewers Guild — once again, using the state's Pure Michigan promotional funds. The program was to work as follows:

Professional recruiting agents, as they were to be called, would visit local brew pubs an hour or so before closing time. They would belly up to the bar and begin to set the mood by playing the country favorite, "I Don't Know Whether to Kill Myself or Go Bowling," on the jukebox dressed in camo and wearing a "Catching 'Em Ain't a Problem — Isn't America Great" T-shirt.

The agent would order a shot and a beer and in a stage whisper inform the barkeep this was in celebration of his take from the day. "What the hell," he would pronounce, "Let's buy a round for all the boys."

Sure enough, after a free shot and a beer, someone would yell, "Hey, fella, thanks for the hit, but what do you mean your 'take' from today?"

The agent, in a faux hushed tone would respond, "Well, I am trying to keep this quiet so as not to saturate the market, but you seem like a good bunch so I will share it with you if you can keep it quiet."

"Sure, we can. What is it?"

"My cousin Kevin, Captain Kevin, runs a charter out of South Haven on a beautiful 42 footer with outriggers, downriggers, unlimited beer and a first mate, Barbara Sue, who was selected as Hooters Girl of the Month last week. Anyways, we have been catching salmon and trout like no tomorrow and selling it to the hoity-toity restaurants that cater to all those city tourists. We call it "natural-organic, non-GMO fish" and are getting $15 a pound for it. Why, I made $350 today, even after paying the charter fees, and did so while spending pounding down craft brews and checking out Barbara Sue while reeling in fish."

At this point, invariably, someone then would quip how that is more than they make in a week and ask, "Is there any way a couple of us can get in on this?" To which the agent would respond, "Well, as I said, I am not supposed to talk about this, but you seem like good guys. Let me call my cousin Kevin and see if he has any room on the 6 a.m. run. We will need the cash up front tonight if by some slim chance he is open, but let me see what I can do. I will give him a call and be back in a minute."

While the recruiting agent is gone, the bartender, who has been prepaid and programmed would chime in, "I've heard of Captain Kevin — told he's the best there is, and he sure lives like a king. Drives a restored '56 Caddy convertible and always has one of those hot blondes you see on the cigarette boats riding shotgun. Hell of a lifestyle, and he only works half a day — whoa, better shut up, here comes that fishing fellow back."

"Okay, boys, talked to Kevin, and you are in luck. He just got a call 30 minutes ago from the Goldman Sachs Chicago office that they need to cancel on their trip in the morning and he has room for eight of you. I will need $100 from each of you up front tonight as an 'overhead fee' to secure a spot and then $100 tomorrow at the boat before launch to cover the 'Maritime Resort Fee.' After that, it is all profit and fun."

Proverbial shooting fish in a barrel. One more round of shots and a beer and all eight pool together $100 a piece while celebrating their newfound luck.

The recruiting agent announces, "Its closing time for me, boys — see you at 6 a.m. sharp at the docks." He slips the barkeep his 10% commission and heads out. Tomorrow will be another day of watching a group of jokers chase fool's gold, but what a job. Perfect work for Bogey and Skeeter.

NINE

F inancially successful in the marijuana import/distribution business, Rosa and Armando lived in a drug-induced fugue state, rarely returning to the world of consciousness. During those rare periods of reality, Rosa would idle away her time posting "likes" on the Facebook page of the Trini Lopez Fan Club, of which she was a member. Armando would usually wile away these short periods by flipping through old discarded editions of *La Gaceta,* the Spanish newspaper, checking the police blotter for recently arrested illegals he could recruit to become part of his sales force in the prison system. He dubbed this activity his "prison outreach program."

One morning, just prior to lighting his start-of-the-day joint, a thin banner ad in *La Gaceta* placed by The Michigan Cannabis Development Association (MCDA) caught his attention. The MCDA, it turns out, was "an organization formed by experienced and knowledgeable business owners with expertise in the medical marijuana field that was formed for the promotion and protection of the Michigan Medical Marijuana Industry." In addition, the mission of the MCDA included the development and support of new businesses to serve as "provisioning centers" to serve all communities, both rural and urban. An aspect of their charge, which had induced the ad, noted they were looking for Spanish-speaking entrepreneurs willing to locate in West Michigan to serve the burgeoning mostly Latin migrant community. The ad assured would-be applicants that an array of state and local incentives would be available for anyone meeting the minimum requirements. Those interested were encouraged to call Battle Creek First for further information and details.

Stoking on his second joint of the day, Armando began to mull the possibilities. This might be their ticket out. Sure, the business had been lucrative, but they surely needed an outlet to launder the cash. He was also concerned that the long arm of the Drug Enforcement Administration (DEA) was on its way. His recent purchase of a 64-foot cigarette boat with cash had not gone unnoticed by the local drug strike force, and this was exacerbated by Rosa insisting on taking an ad in the *Hemp Times* underground paper looking for a "rural landing strip with night lights" on an as-needed basis. Armando knew it was only a matter of time before the law would begin to close in on them, and they needed a new gig.

"Rosa, we need to look into this new opportunity in Michigan. I saw an ad in *La Gaceta* yesterday that might pave the way for us to become involved in the growing $5 billion medical marijuana business," coaxed Armando as they sped across the causeway to St. Pete with the top down on his new Maserati. "I'm afraid the feds might be onto us, and it will be hard to explain some of our recent purchases with our only visible income being my part-time job as a busboy at the Columbia Restaurant. Plus, this might be a way for us to enter the legit economy using the only skill set we have. What do you think?"

"I think you have lost your fricking mind," responded Rosa while toking away on her fourth hit of the day. "What legit business could we possibly run? The only thing we know how to do is roll and sell joints, plus there is a lot of snow up there, and it is not the kind you blow up your nose."

"Don't be so negative. We have extensive experience in sales, finance, marketing and distribution. Shit, we could practically run General Motors! Why, I remember a few years ago, you made weed infused Toll House chocolate chip cookies that sold better than the Girl Scout stuff. We could start a medical marijuana bakery with a whole array of products. You will be known as the queen of confection, and we will become pillars of the community, all paid for by the government."

"What about the snow? I have never been north of Gainesville."

"Just think climate change," assured Armando. "We will be ahead of the curve. No more stifling summers in Tampa, and with the rate of change by the time we get to

Michigan, snow will probably be a thing of the past. What do you say?"

"You're an idiot, but go ahead and call the damn number. Just don't commit to anything."

"Love ya, baby," exclaimed Armando.

TEN

J aap was getting concerned. He had spent the last eight and half years with a death grip on the government tit and now this term-limit rule was about to derail his gravy train. The term-limit issue had been a great issue to run on — red meat for his evangelical, Tea Party base — especially when he had been assured by the Senate Majority Leader that legislation would be slipped through nullifying implementation before it would affect him. A plan which, unfortunately for Jaap, was sidetracked when the Majority Leader was forced to resign after using his state-owned credit cards on a trip to Florida for something called "the full body massage package" at an establishment called the Booby Bungalow. Now Jaap, the conservative, faith-based, pro-free enterprise advocate, faced the terrifying prospect of having to earn a living in the private sector.

His daily one and half hour drive from Holland to Lansing, the state capital, gave Jaap plenty of time to reflect and usually included a stop at his favorite coffee shop, Biggby's, in Zeeland. Always the gregarious, glad-handing politician, he knew them, and they knew him.

"Hey, Jaap — your regular double latte?" chirped Bippy, the young Grand Valley University college student barrister as he sauntered in.

"Sure enough, and give me a blueberry muffin with it. Why, my district is one of the largest producers of blue-berries in the country, and I believe in supporting local farmers."

Bippy had heard this same line countless times, but he tipped pretty well so she just acted like it was some-thing new each time he came in by remarking, "I didn't know that."

"How's business, Bippy?" he would always ask.

Each time she would change her response just to keep the banter fresh. "Strong. People will pay about anything for coffee. Prostitution may be the oldest profession, but there is no question selling addictive caffeine is the most profitable. Look at these prices — $4.25 for a 12-ounce coffee that costs about 5 cents for the liquid and 2 cents for the cup. Why, the margins are off the charts. Hell, if someone could figure out a way to combine sex with java, they would be set for life."

That little girl might be onto something, thought Jaap as he mulled over what he had just heard continuing his drive to Lansing. What a combo, legally addictive coffee with a shot of lewdness thrown in. How to put the two together would require some ingenuity, but even if he figured out an angle, he had no money or the know-how to even start a lemonade stand, much less a real business. All the while, Berdenna was burning through his senate salary by enrolling in every late-night weight-reduction scheme being hustled on reruns of *Dallas* and then outfitting herself at the "Full Woman Boutique" across from Dunkin' Donuts. Combined with normal expenses, it left little of his meager Senate salary despite managing to eat and drink for free for the past eight years, courtesy of the capitol lobby corps.

The cell phone broke his chain of thought. "Jaap, darling." It was Berdenna. "We have just received an invitation for an event tomorrow night with an organization with the acronym COYOTE. It is from 7:00 to 9:00 at the Radisson Hotel, and it says if guests want to stay later they may do so for a small 'service fee.' What in the world could this be? Are coyotes an endangered species?"

"Must be. I will have the staff check it out, but if it is from 7 to 9 p.m., that means heavy hors d'oeuvres and an open bar, so we will probably want to go. Just don't wear any fur, since I imagine it will include a bevy of animal-rights activists."

"Okay, I will dress accordingly. I just hope they have gift bags when you leave. These types of events usually have a two-for-one coupon for Kilwins Fudge Shop."

As Chairman of the Appropriations Subcommittee on Economic Development, Jaap was invited to almost every trade association function in Lansing. Often he would attend not even knowing who they were or what they were about. Lately, however, with his term coming to a close, the invitation stack was getting smaller and smaller. This worried him since lobbyist largesse was a form of supplemental income very much in need. Free food and booze was part of the job and maybe at one of these events he might get an inspiration of what to do next.

Every weeknight there would be numerous events at the Radisson, and Jaap and Berdenna would make the rounds, sometimes even uninvited. Belly up to the bar, work the buffet line and grab a gift bag before driving back to Holland. The night of the COYOTE event, it had totally slipped his mind to have the staff check it out, but no matter, it was pretty obvious it was some sort of animal rights group, and why not stop by for a quick martini and a free meal? Arriving at the reception desk, he noticed only one other senator was in attendance, Senator Jack Tool, a Democrat minister from Saginaw. Strange, he thought there weren't more legislators attending.

Greeting them was a 30ish Asian woman in hot pants, a halter top, four-inch heels and a name tag identifying her as "Monique — the ringmaster of love." The only corporate sponsor evident was a banner behind the table extolling "Trixie's Pole Dancing School — You Have What It Takes." Jaap, upon entering the ballroom, was startled to see the room was filled with women similarly attired as Monique, and when he made eye contact with Senator Tool, the reverend minister beat it out the back door.

"Berdenna, there is something different about this event. It is not the usual bedraggled group of animal-rights activists in Birkenstocks, flannel shirts and cargo pants."

"I agree. Sure is a lot of skin showing. Maybe it is the naturists society, you know advocates for nudity, trying to expand their base by looking after endangered wildlife to make themselves more legit."

"Regardless, let's beeline it to the bar, get a to-go cup, grab some of the dog-in-a-bun appetizers and get the hell out of here. This is political dynamite if I get caught here."

Just about this time, a buxom blonde with a name tag identifying her as "Dreamy from Climax, Michigan" saddled up to Jaap causing him to pitch forward with his martini spilling right on to her décolletage.

"So sorry," he exclaimed.

"No problem," she responded. "It happens all the time. I just wanted to introduce myself. I am the new President of COYOTE and head of our legislative outreach program. COYOTE as you probably know stands for Call Off Your Old Tired Ethics and we are the official association, now union, of prostitutes. Our legislative agenda includes pension reform, health care and most important, performance bonuses. In addition, we have exciting news to share with you. After only one night with the President of the Service Employees International Union (SEIU), I was able to secure our organization the designation as an affiliate member of the SEIU. The only difference between us and our brothers and sisters in the labor movement — considering our lack of attire, we are not called 'card-carrying members,' but rather 'new economy members.' By the way, being new economy members, we think it's great since it allows us to expand our services to all sorts of workplaces where our skills are in demand. Would it be possible for me and a couple of my colleagues to stop by your office sometime?"

"Well, uh, sure, but my schedule is very busy, but I will tell my appointment secretary to expect your call."

Berdenna, mouth agape, stood speechless. This was a long way from the Junior League of Holland, but deep down inside, she was jealous as hell. She had as much stuff to strut as any of these hookers, yet they were making big bucks and she was facing life with an unemployed former politician. She thought back to her Business 101 Class at Calvin College where the professor had emphasized asset management. Why, she had two of the biggest assets in the room and a pretty hot set of wheels to match. Now she just had to figure out how to put them to use.

"Berdenna, pay attention. We need to get the hell out of here. Grab some of those spring rolls. I'll get two more martinis for the road and we can hustle out that back door Senator Tool used. If stopped by the press, we will explain our presence as fulfilling our evangelical responsibility to reach out to wayward souls."

ELEVEN

Bucolic Glenn, the Pancake Town. Named as such on the basis of an episode in the 1930s when ostensibly hundreds of motorists were stranded there in a snowstorm and were forced to survive on pancakes. Never mind they had eggs, flour, milk and all the other fixings. It is a story, probably embellished with age, that is repeated by the local real estate hustlers to imbue an aura of charm and simple values to would-be customers from Chicago and Detroit.

The glistening Lake Michigan waters, sandy beaches, blueberry fields, vineyards and a smattering of horse farms on rolling hills create an ambiance of environmental peace and harmony. Not much more than a general store, diner and hardware store along with a one-room school house constitute the perfect getaway from the noise and congestion of the big city. Why, it even has a bandstand that looks like it is ready for John Philip Sousa to arrive. A Norman Rockwell town on steroids.

Strange place for Red to be taking the top executives of ERR, except for one very dirty little secret. Turns out, there was a time when some residents of Glenn had visions of this area of Michigan becoming the Midwest version of East Texas.

In the late 1950s, Claude VanDerBeek established a gas station on the outskirts of Glenn on what is now an abandoned golf course. He anticipated having a monopoly on the north/south lakeshore traffic, which would allow him to double and triple charge for everything from gas and batteries to repairs. He even went so far as to apply for and obtain oil drilling rights, thinking, who knows, maybe there was some of that black bubbly right beneath him. Permit in hand, he attempted drilling once or twice but soon realized, to his chagrin, that the black goo he was pulling up was only the oil wastes he was secretly dumping in the creek behind the station. The business itself never really took off, and its eventual demise was cemented when it was determined that a new interstate highway would be built a few miles away on land owned by the sister of the local state senator. Claude eventually sold the business and adjoining land "with all water and mineral rights thereto" to his second cousin twice removed, Jack VanDerLaan. Jack, who had never broken 100, declared he was going to build a golf course that soon would be known as the Augusta of the North, both in quality and decorum. The latter being so important that the scorecards required "that shirts be worn on holes 1, 9, 10 and 18" since they fronted the road. He made a go of it until an ugly scene one night put a serious damper on the course's image and revenues. It was a league night, and a brawl broke out between the South Haven Moose Lodge and the Bangor VFW over a disputed raffle ticket for a case of Schlitz Beer. Chairs flew, windows broke, tables were smashed and all the plastic forks and spoons were stolen. The local sheriff, whose brother owned a competing golf course, declared a countywide state of emergency and arrested over 20 participants, including the two hookers who had been hired to tend the pins on holes 5 and 13. The physical damage was significant, and the timing could not have been worse since Jack had just instituted a major billboard advertising campaign touting his facility as "the family friendly course." Facing major repair costs and a tarnished image, he was financially ruined and abandoned the property and moved to Florida, where he sold timeshares in July and August to snowbirds who wanted "a piece of the action."

Red had stumbled upon these historical notes of Glenn while watching a 15-minute late night show on the community cable channel entitled "A Comprehensive Overview of Dutch Entrepreneurs and Their Contributions to Economic Growth and Job Creation in Our State." Always an advocate for the underdog, this little bit of history had stuck with him, and now he could put it to good use for ERR LLC, Boone Cartwright and maybe even for himself.

"I think this location in Glenn will be a perfect area for you to invest. The local government is very weak and malleable. The area qualifies under the 'needy neighborhood provision' for job training, and the abandoned golf course qualifies for restoration funds under the Rebuild Michigan Program. Also Montavious, back to your question about Native Americans. Not only do they receive special treatment for job training but their employment can be subsidized under the Native American Restoration Act implemented through the Michigan Department of Labor. Simply put, this can be a turnkey operation with little or no money up front," briefed Red as they closed in on Glenn.

"Young man, that sounds like an ideal opportunity for my company," exclaimed Boone. "Ron, what do you think?

"I agree with you, sir."

"Montavious, what about you?"

"Hiring Native Americans would garner a lot of points for us with the Equal Employment Opportunity Commission (EEOC) under our court-ordered Diversity Awareness Program. Why, we could put pictures of people wearing headdresses and living in tepees in our annual report to show the company's sensitivity to cultural awareness."

"Brooke, your thoughts?"

"I'm cold. When does the Caribbean affect kick in?"

"Don't worry, we are almost there," assured Red.

Two-lane state road 43 cuts through the countryside and a few small towns before intersecting with another two-lane road known as the Blue Star Highway in South

Haven. Turning right there, headed north, Red, with Boone, Brooke, Montavious and Ron cruised through another 10 miles or so of the countryside until entering Glenn and coming upon an overgrown field with a couple of dilapidated buildings and a shotgun blasted sign announcing you have arrived at *"Glenn National Golf Links: A Family Friendly Course Where Memories Are Made."*

From the looks of it, bad memories. It was bleak. A dilapidated, collapsing clubhouse and what appeared to be an abandoned storage barn with a rusted tractor and mower, a 1950-ish snowmobile with some kind of trailer contraption attached with weeds growing throughout and empty gas cans and plastic Roundup dispensers strewn about. So bad even the mice and snakes would have second thoughts about living there. The only aspect not totally forlorn was a relatively new sign by Torch Reality advertising "Retired Golf Course Lots Available."

Red pulled the Escalade onto the gravel road that had been the main entrance so that they could overlook the scene. His passengers were silent — not a good omen. He would need to put some spin on this, and quickly if he was going to keep their interest.

"Okay, everybody, let's hop out of the car. I want to show you something. Don't pay any attention to the condition of the land or facilities. Blight removal is always a plus in economic development. The worse the blight, the greater the incentives. We just need to take a stroll over to that storage shed."

"I hope my heels don't get stuck in the mud," fretted Brooke. "My shoes are Manolo Blahnik."

"No worry, we don't have far to go, and the little jewel we are looking for is right behind that shed. All the rest of this, the land, the buildings, is gravy," assured Red.

The five of them waded through the mud and knee-high grass and straight into a 28 mph wind, which in 35-degree temperature made for a wind chill of minus 10 degrees. After about a quarter mile, they stopped behind the old storage shed where a corroded lonely pipe stood out of the ground about a foot high.

"There it is. The original drilling pipe installed by Mr. VanDerBeek almost 60 years ago when he was looking for oil. This drilling facility clearly constitutes a renewable resource under any reasonable interpretation of the tax code. Why, with a little bit of attention this site could become a national model of restoration and job creation. A shining example of how free enterprise can simul-taneously address our national energy concerns while rebuilding a communty in an environmentally sustainable manner, and it can all be done with government money," exclaimed Red.

"You mean this will cost us nothing?" Boone replied.

"Nada," responded Red.

"What do you think Montavious?" asked Boone.

"Bourgeois repositioning," he responded.

"Ron?"

"Whatever you say," he replied.

"Brooke?"

"I'm cold."

"Okay Red, put us a package together. No ERR money upfront, no claw-back provisions, no job commitments, no permitting issues and we need the whole package approved within 30 days, right Ron?"

"Right," responded Ron.

Red: "Done."

TWELVE

T he Animals hit song "House of the Rising Sun" had a refrain "and it's been the ruin of many a poor boy," which in the case of Paddy and Sean could apply to their newly acquired addiction to foosball. They were practically residents of that gin joint, The Library, where the table was located. They would spend mindless hours hunched over the foosball game with pitchers of beer, taking on all comers, and if you kept winning, the challengers had to pay so it was all free. Sean even went to far as to create a fantasy foosball league — dubbed the National Foosball League or NFL which was fine and good until he posted on Facebook that The Library was hosting NFL night and that all the league stars, "those players you always wanted to meet," would be in attendance sharing tips and signing autographs. Word got out among the jocks on campus, and the entire football, baseball, hockey and most of the wrestling team came for the big event expecting to see famous football players from the NFL, as in football, only to find nine nerds with pocket protectors discussing shot ratios from different player positions on the foosball "field." Sean was admitted that evening to the emergency room "with severe bruising under the eyes, a dislocated shoulder, welts over his body and a traumatic head injury." The Library itself suffered modest damage to chairs and windows, but did declare that henceforth the National Foosball League would no longer be welcome as a result of the melee that broke out when the college jocks realized that they had been duped.

The incident at The Library had been a setback, but Paddy and Sean had another problem. They were flunking out. Despite taking the easiest courses and the minimum number of hours, all that beer and foosball had taken its toll.

"I just got a notice from Father Doyle that I have been put on double probation and that if I miss one more class, I am out of here," lamented Sean while sipping his third Guinness for lunch.

"Those guys have got to learn how to take a joke," quipped Paddy, one beer behind Sean. "I received a similar warning from Father Ryan regarding his class on 'Cultural Barriers to Political Assimilation and Civic Empowerment.'"

Sean: "What the hell is that course about?"

Paddy: "If you are poor, you're screwed."

Sean: "Well, we have to do something or we are toast. I can't stand the idea of getting booted and having to go back to the South Side. First, my old man will beat the shit out of me. Secondly, my mother will start wailing and screaming about praying to St. Jude, the saint of the impossible, being my only hope. Finally, I will have to go back to Alderman Fitzpatrick, hat in hand, asking him if he can help me get my old job back counting cars for the Cook County Road Commission."

Paddy: "Yeah, that sucks. Here is an idea, though. How about we approach Fathers Ryan and Doyle with the notion that our time in The Library was actually part of an independent study combined research project of our two disciplines, Poly Sci and Criminal Justice, looking into the societal and political ramifications of alcohol and its impact on crime and community norms. What do you think?"

Sean: "Bullshit."

Paddy: "What do you mean bullshit?"

Sean: "Exactly that — they would say bullshit. Hell, Father Doyle is in The Library practically every night from 7 to 9, and he knows all we do is drink beer, play foosball and futilely hit on that waitress with the "Dream On" tattoo on her stomach. We need to come up with something better than that."

Paddy: "Okay, how about this one. We leave before they ask us to leave. I read in *People* magazine that President Obama's daughter took a gap year before going to college. Why don't we propose we take a gap year in the middle of college? Hell, this could be trend setting. We might end up in *People* magazine."

Sean: "Waitress, another beer."

Paddy: "I even know what we might do. I saw a notice on the Poly Sci bulletin board the other day about a state senator in Michigan who was looking for a couple college interns ready to begin working immediately."

Sean: "What would we be doing?"

Paddy: "I don't know. Typical intern stuff, I guess. You know — answer the phone, drive the car, run errands. Run-of-the-mill gofer stuff. Just think, though, at night all those lobbyist parties with free food, booze and where you get to purport to be something more important than what you are all the time, eating and drinking for free. The more I think about it, I believe we would really be good at it. Plus, we could spin it back home with our parents that being selected for these coveted positions was in recognition of our academic accomplishments."

Sean: "Sure, all this sounds great, but we are two guys about to flunk out of college and we don't know anyone in Michigan, so just exactly how do we get these jobs?"

Paddy: "Oh yes, we do know someone in Michigan. My second cousin Danny, who is a bartender at the Watering Hole Lounge in East Lansing, owes me $200. I posted bond for him after he was arrested for burning a couch in a riot following the Michigan State University victory over University of Michigan in football. His dad, Jack Maguire, is a big-time lobbyist in Lansing who represents the Craft Brewers Guild and gives away a lot of money. He will know the state senator. I will tell Danny we are even on the $200 bucks if he can get his dad to get us this gig. It's a no-brainer."

Sean: "What is the name of this state senator?"

Paddy: "Jaap VanValkenberg."

Sean: "Waiter, two more beers."

THIRTEEN

"**T**ank you veddy much, my name Rick — click."

Skeeter: "Why did you hang up?"

Bogey: "Must have been a wrong number. Some Indian dude."

Skeeter: "Dot or feather?"

Bogey: "Dot."

Skeeter: "Try it again 1-800-MIS-FITS."

"Tank you veddy much, my name Rick, welcome to the Michigan Unemployable Hotline. Your name, please?"

"My name is Bogey Jackson, and I am here with my buddy Skeeter Williams. We are calling about the ad in *Field and Stream* for adventure seekers. Where the hell are you?"

"Ganges."

"India?"

"No, Michigan."

"Where is Ganges near?"

"Glenn."

"Where is Glenn near?"

"Nowhere."

"You're shittin' me!"

"No, my name Rick."

"Okay, I give up. Tell us about these jobs."

"Veddy sought-after positions. Must have love of outdoors and be familiar with grain-based products. Whole of West Michigan loves grain-based products. Why popular cereal companies do business there. First, must see if you qualified. Do you drink beer?"

Bogey: "Hell, yes — does a bear shit in the forest?" Why, me and Skeeter have five DUI's between us. We have a proven track record."

"You veddy qualified in that category. Now, do you get seasick?"

Bogey: "Neither one of us has ever been on the ocean, but we fish all the time on Catfish Lake and only get sick if we eat what we catch. And one of my favorite shows is reruns of *Sea Hunt* with Lloyd Bridges on the Adventure Channel."

"You sound very qualified in that category. Do you have any sales experience?"

Bogey: "Well, sort of. Skeeter here sold his grandmother a bill of goods and got her to invest in an outdoor concert venue in Hahira below the gnat line after I sold Skeeter on the notion he should go after the old gal's money. Two slick sales job, if I might say."

"You sound veddy qualified in that category. Finally, veddy important question. Do you have degrees?"

Bogey: "Sure enough. My man Skeeter passed the advanced training course at Critter Control while working on his GED, and I was selected as Technician of the Month at the Hahira Jiffy Lube and just last week sent in my money for the Dale Carnegie TV special, Silver Platinum Correspondence Course. Most important, my dead Uncle Lindsay says we both have degrees from the school of hard knocks."

"You sound veddy qualified in this category. You have successfully passed all the requirements for the Make West Michigan Grow Program."

Bogey: "Wow, that is exciting news. How many others will be in our group?"

"Just the two of you."

Bogey: "How many have gone through this program before?"

"Just the two of you."

Bogey: "In three years?"

"Yes, veddy select program."

Bogey: "Damn, wait till they hear about this in Hahira. And they said we wouldn't amount to nuthin'. How much do we get paid?"

"You paid $7.25 an hour plus commission. With any luck you make six figures within a year. First, you must report for job training and assignment at Battle Creek First, 2 West Michigan Avenue, Battle Creek, Michigan. Ask for Red Johansson. Tank you veddy much for calling the Michigan Unemployable Hotline."

Bogey: "Damn Skeeter, we may have hit the big time, but where the fuck is Battle Creek, Michigan?"

Skeeter: "I have no idea, but did you not know that Michigan has the second longest coastline in the U.S. second only to Alaska?"

Bogey: "What the hell does that have to do with where is Battle Creek?"

Skeeter: "I don't know nuthin', I guess."

Bogey and Skeeter immediately took on a new persona as word spread about their new jobs and as they prepared for the journey up north. They announced to anyone who would listen that they had taken executive positions in the outdoor adventure travel business and were being relocated to a turnaround region in recognition of their unique skill sets.

The trip up north would require a great deal of planning and preparation considering neither one of them had ever been farther north than Tennessee. First, for music and their triumphant departure in the F-150 pickup, they acquired a knock-off eight-track tape of that country classic, "Get Your Tongue Outta My Mouth Cause I'm Kissing You Goodbye." Skeeter "borrowed" his cousin's cooler from his back porch, along with two cases of Bud Light left over from the weekend drag races. Bogey was able to counterfeit a Premium Costco Card, which would allow them to stop for free food at the store sampling stations as they made the trek north. No detail was too small. In anticipation of the Costco visits, they had quart

Ziplock bags installed in the pockets of their camo jackets to hold the pilfered food. Holiday Inns were identified with ice makers in the hallways where the cooler could be refilled and, of course, the ubiquitous McDonald's would fulfill its role as America's bathroom. Why, with any luck, they would make it from Hahira to Battle Creek on the cost of gas and beer alone.

Skeeter: "Bogey, one thing I am going to sure miss is Waffle House. I don't think they have any of them up north."

Bogey: "Probably not. The only thing I have ever heard of Yankee's eating is rhubarb, and there sure as hell ain't any rhubarb on the menu at Waffle House."

Skeeter: "Well before we blow out of town, we need to go see Norma Jean at the Exit 38 Waffle House. By the way, did you know that the busiest day at a Waffle House is Christmas Day?"

Bogey: "What does that have to do with anything?"

Skeeter: "Nuthin, I guess."

Bogey: "You're an idiot."

Bogey and Skeeter loved Norma Jean. Norma Jean Boatmen pretended to listen when they talked and, too many times to count, had pumped them full of coffee so they could make that early morning two sheets to the wind drive home.

Norma Jean glanced up from taking an order when they arrived late morning and gave a shout, "Hey fellas, be right with you. Understand you got some big news." She sauntered over to the table wearing her official Waffle

House waitress uniform, which had been modified to show as much cleavage and leg as possible. She called it her tip inducement outfit.

Norma Jean: "Hey, guys, what can I get you?"

Skeeter: "I will have the All-Star Special."

Bogey: "Make that two."

Norma Jean: "You got it," and shouts out the order: "Pull one bacon, drop one hash brown scattered, smothered and loaded. Mark order scramble plate, bacon and a waffle."

Skeeter: "Can you top off my coffee?"

Norma Jean: "You betcha."

Norma Jean's name was really Beth Boatman, but she found her tips went up when she had a Southern double name. She had worked at the Waffle House for 10 years and her mother had worked here before for 30 years. The Waffle House was her home, and the customers were her family. Even wayward ones like Bogey and Skeeter.

Norma Jean: "Word is that the two of you have lined up jobs as outdoor travel guides. Amazing! How did you come across this?"

Skeeter: "We spotted an ad in *Field and Stream* and then went through a rigorous interview with some Indian dude in Ganges."

Norma Jean: "India?"

Skeeter: "No, Michigan."

Norma Jean: "Sounds kind of crazy. Hope it all works out for you, but I guess nothing to lose. Nothing but a dead end here."

Bogey: "Thanks Norma Jean. You're the best. They say we will be making six figures in no time and when we do, we won't forget you!"

Norma Jean: "Well, good luck up there. Never been up north, but have a third cousin, Mary Sue Canoe, who works as a waitress in a restaurant called the What Knot Inn."

Bogey: "Is her name really Mary Sue Canoe?"

Norma Jean: "Nope, it is Matilda, but she gets better tips if she uses a double Southern name."

Skeeter: "This would be wild, but any chance the restaurant is in either Ganges or Battle Creek?"

Norma Jean: "Nope, it is some place called Glenn."

FOURTEEN

"Rosa why don't you call these guys at Battle Creek First," suggested Armando.

"Why me? This is your crazy idea, and what am I going to say if I do?" she replied.

"I have an idea how we can get them to fund our medical marijuana bakery, and it goes back to when you were a Girl Scout."

"Girl Scout! What the hell are you talking about? I only lasted one week before Sister Domenico gave me the boot for posting nude selfies on my Facebook page in my attempt to earn a 'making new friends badge.'"

"No problem — one week can have a lasting impact on your life. Okay, here's the plan"

"Hello, thank you for calling Battle Creek First where customer care and courtesy are job one. My name is Isabella. What do you want?"

"Hola, Isabella. My name is Rosa Castellano, and I am calling in regard to an ad that appeared in *La Gaceta* here in Tampa about provisional centers for medical marijuana to serve the Latin community of West Michigan. Are you the one I should speak with?"

"What the hell is *La Gaceta?*"

"It is the Spanish newspaper located in Tampa, Florida. Quite renowned."

"God save us. What next? No, you need to speak with Red Johansson, our president, who personally runs that program. Let me see if he is in."

"Hey, Red, I've got some immigrant on line two inquiring about the Michigan Cannabis Development Association Account. Something about a Latin Outreach Program and with that name and accent, she clearly qualifies."

This was the first call he had received for the Association in months. The last one was from a guy named Hector Garcia calling from the Jackson State Prison, where he was doing 20 years to life for cocaine smuggling. Hector thought an effort to enter the private sector would help his chances at his next parole hearing. Red attempted to return the call but never heard back. Turns out that Hector's parole hearing was cancelled and he was put in solitary for stabbing a fellow inmate over whether to listen to Christian music or rap on the community radio.

Red thought the whole Cannabis Association initiative was total nonsense, but they paid Battle Creek First a nice monthly retainer for doing essentially nothing, which in turn allowed him to pad his salary under an auxiliary account-management provision. Eager to keep the account alive, he figured why not talk to her. If nothing else, it would give him something to put in the account activity ledger in his monthly board report and in the quarterly update to the Association. Plus, he could also use it as a sop to Senator VanValkenberg, who was always on his case for not directing more projects to his district in West Michigan.

"Okay, Isabella, put her on, but if the conversation goes on for more than ten minutes come in and loudly announce that my next meeting is waiting so I can get off with her."

"Sí, Señor," replied a sarcastic Isabella.

"Ms. Castellano, I am transferring you to Mr. Johansson."

"Hi, Red Johansson here. What can I do for you?"

"My name is Rosa Castellano, and I am calling about the ad by the Michigan Cannabis Development Association and their Latin Outreach Program. I believe I am ideally suited for this program and that it will enable me to become a philanthropic Ganjapreneur working with under-resourced communities in partnership with government, faith-based institutions, business and other non-government organizations involved in civic engagement."

"Keep talking Rosa, you've got my attention."

"My interest in help creating a new charitable model of Ganjapreneur is derived from the tenets of my Catholic Christian upbringing and the school motto at the Academy of the Holy Names 'give what you got!' Simply put, my role in this endeavor will be directed by divine guidance."

Red's head was spinning. This was too good to be true. A Latin skirt (two points!) appearing in front of Senator VanValkenberg's Economic Development Subcommittee espousing Christian values as the basis for a new business in his district. Why, 'ol Jaap will put together an incentive package for this one in a nanosecond, and it can be bundled with Boone and the oil boys. Come to think of it, this might be the opportunity I have been looking for to slip a little bit for me in an omnibus legislative proposal. God knows I need it to get Ingrid off my back about my paltry salary from Battle Creek First.

"Rosa, I find this all fascinating. Tell me a little bit more about what you envision?"

"It will be a medical marijuana bakery serving the needs of low-income citizens. The idea first came to me when I was a Girl Scout selling cookies. I kept thinking how much good I could do if the cookies came with added value, and what better value than substituting health for fat and sugar. Why, they could even be made with non-GMO water. In addition, my business partner, Armando, thought we might be able to do a direct tie-in with the Girl Scouts making them part of their sales portfolio and thereby keeping distribution costs down. Just imagine packaging with the Girl Scouts' trefoil overlapping a marijuana leaf. This could be big."

Red couldn't believe what he was hearing. This was too good to be true. An economic incentive involving

Latin, Christian, philanthropy and now the Girl Scouts. Getting a package for this would be a no-brainer.

"Okay, sweetheart, I like what I am hearing. But what is the catch?"

"Well, we don't have any money."

"That's all?"

"Yes, Mr. Johansson — just money — a material barrier we should not let stand in the Lord's way."

"I agree, and I assure you that you have come to the right place. We revere the free market and capitalism here in West Michigan, and that is why we have set up numerous government programs to help would-be Ganjapreneurs such as yourself to get started. Now, I must caution you that all applications for economic incentives are judged solely on merit, but you being Latin and female is almost a shoo-in. You don't have any Indian heritage do you?"

"My great grandfather was a native of Cuba."

"Perfect, native blood — this is almost a done deal. I even have an idea for what might be a good location, but one last issue. Would you be willing to come up and testify before the Senate Subcommittee on Economic Development and lay out what you just told me? They are the ones that approve economic incentive packages."

"No problem. I was described as the queen of embellishment in my high school yearbook."

"Just curious — what do you plan to call this medical marijuana bakery?"

"Apothecary Gobbles."

"How does Glenn Apothecary Gobbles sound?"

"Sounds good to me."

"Rosa you're talking with your new business partner. I will be back in touch."

FIFTEEN

All was not copacetic in the Johansson household. Nine years at Battle Creek First had been a backwater for Red's career. It looked like the Corvette he envisioned when he signed up for the Economic Developer Correspondence Course was simply a mirage. Sure, the pay was okay, but never really enough to compensate for having to put up with the steady flow of corporate drones he had to suck up to, and his feelings of ennui was only exasperated by Ingrid's recent religious conversion.

"You are his infidel," she would scream at him each night as he came through the front door of their modest split-level. He would get a bracer for this daily occurrence by stopping by The Gentleman's Lounge, a.k.a. the last stop before home, for a pop or two. Usually a Double Hop Ale is with a shot or two, but even this wasn't enough to take the edge off.

Ingrid had become radicalized in a New Age church called The Path Forward, which espoused Christian capitalism and studied the teachings of John D. Rockefeller.

She had been enticed to join this congregation by her yoga teacher, Fran Vanderbeek, who had started the church in an abandoned strip mall. The fundamental tenet of the religion was based on **1 Timothy 5:8:** *But if any provide not for his own, and especially for those of his own house, he hath denied the faith, and is worse than the infidel."*

This was translated by yoga teacher, the Reverend Fran Vanderbeek to the exclusively female congregation to raise the question, Was your husband a deadbeat? She would then excoriate her parishioners that it was their duty, as tools of the Lord, to provide motivation for their husbands to seek enrichment, and by doing so they would fulfill themselves in the eyes of their creator. It was also incumbent upon them to tithe this newfound wealth to keep the mission of the church alive.

The nagging that came with this religious conversion would have been completely untenable except for the fact as far as family finances were concerned, she was not all wrong. The Johansson's balance sheet was pitiful. Not exactly down and out, but nowhere near where they thought they would be when they started this gig. Red would mull over the irony of how he had spent a career getting the government to give money to rich people in the form of incentives to make them richer while people like him in the middle class got nothing. If only he was a National Football League or Major League Baseball team owner, he could get the government to give him hundreds of millions of dollars and watch taxpayers do it with glee!

Somewhere he thought to himself, in the mix of new businesses he would be pitching in Lansing, there had to be a handle for him and Ingrid to get a piece of the action. Somehow that shiny new Corvette would become a reality. Someday he would become management and enjoy the fruits of government-subsidized capitalism where those who do the least get the most.

Three beers were usually his limit at The Gentlemen's Lounge, but Red was already on his fourth and not quite ready to go home. Today at the office had been a real slog as he prepared to meet tomorrow with Senator VanValkenberg to discuss his list of potential prospects and prepare for the subcommittee's hearing on West Michigan Economic Activity. He had distilled his list for state licensing an attendant funding to four main projects, which also conveniently covered a wide swath of constituent interests of the five-member subcommittee. Pork politics have always been the key to getting a package approved and the only thing better than taking care of constituents was taking care of the members themselves. Why, only last week when another subcommittee chair was ambushed by the local television station and accused of having a conflict of interest for funding his daughter's dog-grooming business in an appropriation for the Humane Society, his retort was, "Doesn't conflict with my interest!" The television reporter stumbled away at a loss for words.

First on the list would be the Environmental Renewable Resource LLC proposal code named <u>Pump It</u>. This would be of great interest to Senator Ten Broeck, who touted himself as an environmental stalwart but who also happened to own a company that made pumps for mining and drilling.

Second on the list would be locating and funding an organization to be called the Outdoor Leisure Inducement Office, code named Bait and Switch. The creation of this group was jointly supported by the Michigan Charter Fisherman's Association and the Michigan Craft Brewers Guild, which just happened to have two of the largest Political Action Committees (PACs) in the state and proudly claimed committee member Senator Huitsma as a wholly owned subsidiary.

Third would be a Hispanic Community Health Center, code named Dreamland, which would eventually be known as the Glenn Apothecary Gobbles Company. Senator Garcia would find this of great interest since his primary source of income was his interest in a home health care company which specialized in free delivery.

Finally, a project of historical significance, strongly supported by the Michigan Tourism Association and its multi-client lobbyist, Jack Maguire, which would create a museum of democracy and civic engagement, code named Jailbird. A clever cover for what would become the National Political Corruption Hall of Fame. A project that would have the backing of Senator Ryksma who whole-heartedly supported anything Jack Maguire wanted so long as he and his 28-year-old confidential assistant, Poppy, had unlimited use of Jack's Panama City, Florida condo.

Not a bad list, but Red had two concerns. Nothing for the chairman. Sure, he had introduced legislation for the National Political Corruption Hall of Fame, but he had really only done it as a favor for Senator Ryksma to give him cover. He had no skin in the game. He needed to figure out something that would take care of the chairman. Most important, however, there was nothing here for him. Once again, left holding the bag.

"Hey, Butch, how about one more beer? Four is usually enough, but after today and what I have tomorrow, a fifth might be in order."

"Coming up — another Double Hop Ale?

"Yeah, and would you hand me that newspaper over there with the headline "Church Hits Pay Dirt?"

"Here you go." Just an old copy of *The National Enquirer*. The lead story was something about that the groundhog was not an endangered species and a court ruling against an environmental group called Save the Groundhog Coalition and in favor of the Church of Resurrection. The coalition immediately filed for relief from the Michigan Supreme Court where five of the nine justices had been supported in their re-election campaigns with six-figure contributions by the Michigan Mining Consortium. The court denied the request, but in so doing determined that the critical factor was not that the ground-hog was or was not an endangered species but rather whether mining, which in this case involved "dynamited crater creation, would be allowed as a matter of local control under the state natural resource law. In this case, the township clerk had approved a request by the church to "reap the bounty of the land." It was irrelevant that the clerk thought the request involved an organic garden. It has been approved, period.

"Butch, give me another beer. I think I just figured out another item for the agenda for my meeting with Senator VanValkenberg tomorrow."

SIXTEEN

The excitement of what he was about to do was almost too much for Red. He was driving to Lansing like a constipated bullfighter — bobbing and weaving between cars and trucks — you would have thought he had a meeting with the Pope rather than Senator VanValkenberg. Come to think of it, though, this meeting was more important than meeting the Pope! Although he had high hopes and was confident he could sell his plan, he had not let Ingrid in on his scheme. No need to build expectations in case it didn't fly.

Mark Twain cautioned, "No man's life, liberty or property are safe while the legislature is in session." So true, but especially so towards the end of a session when "must do" bills and appropriations have to be passed. The convergence of these "must do" items usually results in a legislative logjam that is cleared by creating an omnibus bill in which everything is thrown together in one bill. An indecipherable mishmash creating an opportune time for mischief, skullduggery and political sleight of hand. Red knew that this appropriation bill out of Senator Van-Valkenberg's subcommittee would get folded into this final catch-all bill. Timing was perfect.

"Hi, Tippy. How are you doing today? I have a 10 o'clock with the senator," Red greeted the senator's receptionist as he entered his legislative office.

"Good to see you, Red. Let me see if he is in," she perfunctorily replied.

Red took a seat in one of the two guest chairs in front of her desk, amused at the "Let me see if he is in" line. Of course, she knew he was in. Hell, the entire office was only two rooms, but it was all part of the charade of power.

"The senator is in. He will be with you in just a few minutes."

"Thanks, Tippy."

Just as he was about to sit down again, out bounded Senator VanValkenberg.

"Good to see you, Red. Thanks for coming up today. You know this will be my last hearing and approps bill, so I want to make it something special and long lasting. Glad you are going to be part of it."

"Well, senator, you are going to be missed, and I will do my best to make this last hearing a fitting tribute to a stellar legislative career and an event neither one of us will ever forget."

"Couldn't agree more, Red. Come on in my office and we can talk about it."

While walking into Dirk's office and shutting the door, Red couldn't help but think about how all the Senate offices looked alike. Pictures of the senator with the most famous people he had met, other politicians and civic leaders from the district along with sundry plaques and awards. Family pictures were a must and, if of the same party, the governor and lieutenant governor. In the case of Senator VanValkenberg, it was Governor Baumgarten, who looked like a cross between the Pillsbury Dough Boy and the Michelin Tire Man.

"Cup of coffee, Red?"

"Sure, thanks."

"Help yourself. We probably better get started. I have a committee meeting at 11 o'clock to discuss designating a new state flower. Very important to the horticulturist community."

"Well, I have four projects, all of which will mean investments and jobs. They are all live ones, but with the competitive environment between the states, we will need some economic incentives and fast-track licensing to make sure we don't lose them. Usual packages, nothing excessive that will create undue media attention. Just enough to make sure we bag them while being consistent with your free-market philosophy without undue government interference."

"Sounds good. Can you give me a quick overview?"

"Sure. The first one is a very exciting environmental oil recovery company from Texas, that we have recruited under the code name Pump It. They employ advanced cutting edge technology to reuse, renew and revitalize natural resources.

The second is something that will be dear to your heart and all of your constituents who hunt and fish. Its code name is Bait and Switch. It will entail a new office located in your district that will encourage collaboration between the budding craft brew industry and charter fisherman. Unprecedented synergy.

The third is a project we call Dreamland, which will address health issues confronting the burgeoning Hispanic population of West Michigan. I anticipate that history will identify this as one of your signature legislative achievements.

Finally, a project called Jailbird, based on your historical understanding that past is prologue. Senator Ryksma has agreed to courageously serve as the primary sponsor of your idea to create a museum dedicated to recognizing the vibrancy and texture of our great nations political infrastructure."

"Red, this is a great list. Do you have witnesses ready and willing to testify on their behalf? The silly press is starting to question why the government is funding so many private businesses. Just shows how naïve they are."

"I am working on that now, but will be good to go when you want us."

"Okay, I will have the clerk put this on the agenda. Let her know who the witnesses will be as soon as you can. The hearing will be in two weeks, and I would like to report the bill out the same day so I can include it in the omnibus bill that goes to the floor the next week. Oh, Red, one last little item. I see where these projects are going to be in and around Glenn. Last time I was there, I noticed a small rural Post Office that had been abandoned. I had my staff look into it and discovered it had been turned over to the Government Surplus Authority. Shame something can't be done with it. Something even as simple as a coffee shop.

"We might be able to help with that. Any ideas?"

"Well, yes, I do. Berdenna and her second cousin Audrey Richenberg have a shell corporation they created years ago called Dutch Girls Make Good, or DGMG Inc., to make and sell wooden shoes to tourists. Audrey is 94, infirmed and in assisted living, which leaves Berdenna as the controlling partner. Of course, we would want to keep everything on the up and up, but for the sake of the town, how about if Battle Creek First were to propose the transfer of the Post Office building to DGMG Inc.? We can just keep it to ourselves who controls the company since we are doing it for the sake of the town and not any personal gain. If we bury it in the subcommittee bill, no one will be the wiser and we can feel good about making a difference."

"Senator, I share your vision and concern. Utilizing existing structures maintains continuity in the community and is environmentally friendly. It is virtuous of you to keep the long-term vitality of Glenn in mind, even as you wind down your political career. Actually, your approach brings to mind one more potential development in the same vein that could fill the spiritual needs of that small town. My Ingrid is in the process of becoming a Universal Life Church Minister through the internet. She has completed a rigorous one-hour course and is anxious to spread the gospel of Christian capitalism. Considering all the new development we are proposing, it would be unchristian to leave the faithful without any place of worship. It occurred to me that the old club house or the abandoned Glenn Golf Course is a property worth preserving. Interestingly, after a cursory review of the property deeds in the county clerk's office, I was able to determine that the old facility is now owned by the state through bankruptcy proceedings. It would be irresponsible to let it go to rack and ruin. Why not legislatively transfer it and all the mineral rights thereto to an organization that can put it to good use. Just so happens Ingrid plans to minister through a nonprofit, faith-based, ecumenical corporation operating as the Wave of the Future Church. This legal entity has an independent Board of Directors consisting of me, Ingrid, a defrocked Catholic Priest and the retired spokesman for the Federal Emergency Management Agency (FEMA) during Katrina under President George W. Bush. You can be assured integrity will never be an issue. Why, with only a sentence or two in the subcommittee bill, you can make all of this happen and in so doing have a meaningful impact on the lives of many."

"Red, you have clearly given this a lot of thought, and it is a worthy cause. Put this in with your subcommittee requests, but make sure DGMG and Wave of the Future are in the addendum, not in the main body. Oftentimes the hearing will run short of time, and we simply incorporate the addendum by reference in the bill even though there has been no public testimony. Probably best we don't confuse the public with too many details if you get my drift."

"Understand completely, senator. My submission with an addendum and witness list will be filed with the clerk in short order."

SEVENTEEN

J aap relished being in the limelight when he chaired a meeting of the Appropriations Subcommittee on Economic Development. This hearing, being his last, would be especially bittersweet. Once the hearing was over and the bill reported out, the accoutrements of power would vanish rapidly. Lobbyists would move on to the next in line for the chairmanship leaving the term-limited solon to fend for himself as far as food and booze were concerned. All the more reason to make sure this last piece of legislation contained some well-deserved benefits for him and Berdenna. It was the least the citizens of Michigan could do for his many years of public service.

"Ladies and gentlemen, the subcommittee will come to order. Clerk, please call the roll"

"Senator Huitsma?"

"Here."

"Senator Ryksma?"

"Here."

"Senator Ten Broeck?"

"Here."

"Senator Garcia?"

"Here."

"Senator VanValkenberg?"

"Here."

"Mr. Chairman, a quorum is present."

"Thank you, clerk. We have a very crowded agenda today, so I will ask the members to forgo opening statements, but the chair would like to make a few remarks seeing as this will be my last as a member of this august body.

First, let me note the addition of two new interns, Sean O'Malley and Paddy Fitzpatrick, who are scholars in the fields of Political Science and Criminal Justice. They will be assisting the subcommittee as we refine, report and implement this legislation.

We as a state are in the vortex of criticality (Jaap had heard Alexander Haig say that, when he was Secretary of State under Ronald Reagan, but despite the fact that Jaap had no idea what it meant, he always thought it sounded intellectual), and it is incumbent on us as stewards of the economy to make sure that our free market is allowed to function free of government entanglement. Too often, less government means more government, requiring us to inject state funds so that unfettered capitalism can flourish. It is with this in mind that we consider the bill before us providing economic incentives for entrepreneurs willing to risk all in the marketplace so long as the state's taxpayers are willing to take the fall if they fail. This can only be considered true economic courage.

We have four witnesses today, and I have asked them to briefly describe their endeavors using the code names assigned to their application so as to preclude any competitive information from leaking. In addition to the four main projects, we have some minor ones listed in the addendum which we can discuss if time allows. I would now like to call the first witness, Mr. Montavious Sharp on behalf of Project Pump It. Welcome, Mr. Sharp."

"Thank you, Mr. Chairman." I am Montavious Sharp, Vice President of Purpose Outreach, Diversity, Inclusion and Cultural Awareness. Our company is a national natural resources company that attempts to revitalize rural and economically challenged communities by recapturing local assets and repositioning them within the flow of commerce. Our company proudly hires same-gender loving people, citizens of advanced age, indigenous Americans, multiracial individuals, non-binary and non-disabled people along with a token white guy now and then. This allows us to proudly proclaim to be an uncompany, mirroring all of humankind."

"Thank you, Mr. Sharp. Are there any questions? Yes, Senator Ryksma."

Senator Ryksma: "Thank you for your testimony. Can you be a little more explicit as to what your company actually will do?"

"Gladly senator. We will reconfigure and reconstitute local economic priorities and assets, which in turn will create an abundance of jobs for historically marginalized groups."

Senator Ryksma: "Thank you, Mr. Sharp. That makes it abundantly clear. No further questions, Mr. Chairman."

"Our next witness is that great American and citizen advocate known to most of us, Mr. Jack Maguire, who is appearing on behalf of the Michigan Tourism Association. Welcome, Mr. Maguire."

"Thank you, Mr. Chairman and members of the subcommittee. It is a pleasure to be here today to discuss project Jailbird. This initiative, if approved by the subcommittee, will have a sweeping effect on tourism. Project Jailbird will capture and memorialize core aspects of our democratic heritage and make those underlying tenets relevant to citizens of all ages. I believe it was Charles de Gaulle who cautioned, "Politics is too important to be left to the politicians," and this project will make clear why this admonition is as true now as it was then. I will not unduly burden you with the details of this undertaking but will assure you that by supporting this proposal, you will leave a lasting imprint for decades to come."

"Are there any questions from the subcommittee for Mr. Maquire? Yes, Senator Ryksma."

Senator Ryksma: "Mr. Maguire, do you still own a condo in Panama City, Florida?"

"Yes, I do, senator."

Senator Ryksma: "No further questions, Mr. Chairman."

"Our next witness is Ms. Rosa Castellano, who will explain Project Dreamland, which portends to be a groundbreaking health outreach strategy directed at the Hispanic and other underserved communities. Welcome, Ms. Castellano."

"Thank you, Mr. Chairman and members of the sub-committee. I come to you as the daughter of immigrants seeking the bounty of America. My great grandfather came from Cuba with only an American Express card and a cigar. He was able to use leverage and mob connections to become an American success story inspiring me to become a Ganjapreneur by creating Project Dreamland. Dreamland will take non-GMO, additive free, fat free, organic, locally grown products and convert them into life changing medicines. Profit is not our objective; happiness is. Our philanthropic mission allows us to work with faith-based institutions and envisions recruiting Girl Scouts as little angels of distribution. Health, happiness and community involvement are the three tenets underpinning Dreamland and a project worthy of taxpayer support."

"Thank you, Ms. Castellano. Are there any questions? Yes, Senator Garcia."

"Ms. Castellano, might Dreamland consider using the infrastructure of the home health care industry as a delivery mechanism?"

"Absolutely, senator. We anticipate using taxpayer dollars to contract with existing home health care companies to serve as agents within the Latin, African American, Native Indian, LBGTQ and Latvian communities."

Senator Garcia: "Thank you, Mr. Chairman. No more questions."

"Our next and final witness is one of the premier economic development professionals and a man known for his integrity and high ethical standards. Welcome, Red Johansson."

"Mr. Chairman and members of the subcommittee, it is an honor and a privilege to appear before you today. I take special note of the fact that this will be Senator Van-Valkenberg's last meeting and that the citizens of this great state are forever indebted to him for his unselfish service and tireless advocacy on behalf of those less fortunate. My organization, Battle Creek First, appreciates all the support the subcommittee has given our efforts over the years. Now you may chuckle when I propose Project Bait and Switch, but it is aptly named since it will be the bait that draws visitors to Southwest Michigan and then they will switch their perceptions of who and what we are all about. Grain-based products and our beautiful blue waters serve as the basis of this tourist inducement program. By supporting Bait and Switch, you will help transform our region into a tourist mecca."

"Thank you, Mr. Johansson. Are there any questions? Yes, Senator Huitsma."

Senator Huitsma: "Mr. Johansson, any chance Project Bait and Switch is supported by the Charter Fisherman's Association and/or craft brewers?"

"Glad you asked, senator. Yes, both organizations enthusiastically support it."

Senator Huitsma: "Well, anything involving beer and pole dancing is something I support. Excuse me, Mr. Chairman, I meant to say a beer and a pole as in fishing, so please revise the record accordingly. No further questions, Mr. Chairman."

"Well, gentlemen, that concludes our witness list for today. Do I hear a motion for adoption of the bill with the addendum?

"Excuse me, Mr. Chairman, I am Matilda Hoffenmeister, Executive Director of the Coalition of Concerned Citizens for Transparent and Ethical Government. I see in the addendum incentives are being proposed for two organizations identified as WOTFC and DGMG Inc. Would you explain to me what those are?"

"Ms. Hoffenmeister, you are clearly out of order. Public notice of the list of projects was made readily available 10 minutes before the hearing. This is not a forum to promote your liberal anti-business agenda. You clearly do not understand legislative protocol, comity and the need to keep confidentiality, or for that matter the free enterprise system. Please be seated. Clerk call the roll."

"Senator Huitsma?"

"Aye."

"Senator Ryksma?"

"Aye."

"Senator Ten Broeck?"

"Aye."

"Senator Garcia?"

"Aye."

"Senator VanValkenberg?"

"Aye."

"Mr. Chairman, by a vote of five ayes and zero no's, the bill is approved and reported."

EIGHTEEN

In the Midwest, a rather large woman might be referred to as a Corn Queen. Governor Earl Baumgarten clearly was deserving of the moniker Corn King. He was obese. A receding hairline, a waddle for a walk and a Taft-like girth, he had a habit of continually using a handkerchief to wipe the sweat from his brow that was impossible to miss. Standing between him and a buffet line was considered the most dangerous spot in Michigan.

Raised on a pig farm in Central Michigan and exposed to the hard work it entailed imbued in him a commitment to avoid any occupation that, as he would quip, involved "heavy lifting" or, in other words, hard work. Never would his name and the word "work" be used in the same sentence. Politics was his calling. Espousing conservative principles despite never having had a real job in the private sector, he was able to secure a death grip on the government tit. As a free-market advocate, railing against big government, he was able to secure a series of jobs on the state payroll — first as a state representative, then senator and finally governor. While in each successive position, he stayed true to his upbringing that pork was a priority.

Now in his second term, the Corn King (aka Handkerchief), like Jaap, was facing the terrifying prospect of entering the real world of the private sector. This term-limited business was a bitch. Luckily, with his appointment powers and a rubber stamp Senate, he had packed every board, commission, council, etc., with the usual array of sycophants, political hacks and obsequious Republican Party officials. The Michigan Economic Development Commission, which was the candy jar of state politics doling out goodies to private business, was no different. The three-member commission, all appointed by ol' Handkerchief consisted of:

Jack Hightower — Executive Director of the Advocacy Group Competition for America, which is an offshoot of the Chamber of Commerce created to promote a business climate unfettered by government interference.

Princess Dancing Bear — A Huron Indian faith healer whose father "Big Slot" owned numerous casinos and was a major contributor to the Baumgarten Victory Fund Super PAC.

And, finally, Sparky Sanchez — who had been the governor's personal trainer until her Weight Watchers franchise was revoked after she was discovered to have a tie-in with Dunkin' Donuts causing a media storm even her minority status could not dissipate.

Now that the legislature had appropriated the money for business recruitment, retention and job creation it was up to this distinguished group to dole out these state resources to deserving businesses with the definition of deserving usually correlating to the size and direction of campaign contributions.

"Ladies and gentlemen, I would like to call this meeting to order. My name is Jack Hightower, and I am the chairman of the Michigan Economic Development Commission and I am joined today by my fellow commissioners Princess Dancing Bear and Sparky Sanchez. We have a quorum and, having such, I officially open the meeting.

"Staff has prepared a list of projects to be considered and since our time is limited, I would ask my fellow commissioners to keep questions to a minimum and allow the staff discretion in implementing the details. We need to be big-picture people, if you know what I mean. Will the Commission Executive Director Barbara Dalrymple identify the projects along with the suggested incentives?"

"Thank you, Mr. Chairman. Let me start by assuring the commission that all of these projects entail standard inducements designed to facilitate job creation and community well-being. None of these projects are a result of political influence, having been selected solely on the merits after having been scrutinized by the legislature in the appropriations process and stripped of any deal breaking clawback provisions. Clawbacks have been deemed by the staff to be inherently unfair. Why should the business be forced to return the benefits if they fail to fulfill the terms of the agreement, e.g. jobs created, investment and so on! Only pesky bureaucrats would worry about such things. Our role is to serve the interests of business — not to become some sort of government nanny. We are quite cognizant of the commission's philosophy that less government is best, except when more is needed. Now to our agenda.

Our first item is Project Dreamland, which for the sake of brevity should be considered a minority health outreach endeavor using cutting-edge medical/pharmaceutical discoveries. Suggested incentives include, inter alia,

$250,000 small business development grant

$300,000 state non-recourse loans

Job training assistance

Job tax credits

$150,000 urban renovation assistance block grant (Glenn qualifies as a town within a 150-mile radius of a city with 10,000 or more people)

Agricultural Renaissance Zone designation, making it tax-free for 15 years

Infrastructure improvements as needed by the town, city, county or state

Promotion assistance

Item number two is Project Bait and Switch. This undertaking utilizes our abundant natural resources in conjunction with grain-based products in a synergistic manner.

$350,000 supplemental assistance grant to hire an executive director

Procurement of a mobile headquarters

Creation of a joint-training program under the auspices of craft brewers and the Charter Fisherman's Organization

Sundry criminal and civil legal services before, during and after inception

Publicity and promotion assistance

Project Pump It is number three on our list. This is a self-funded environmental initiative simply requiring expedited land transfers and permitting in keeping with the governor's exhortation, "The snail darter be damned."

Transfer of abandoned property under the Rural Reclamation Act

Creation of a no-enforcement zone by the Department of Natural Resources

Double bonus tax credit for hiring under the Department of Labor's Disadvantaged, Ethnically Challenged and Culturally Marginalized Worker Program

Extending and repaving the runway at the community airport to accommodate a Falcon 900 Jet

Item number four is Project Jailbird, destined to become a major tourist attraction. This will also serve as a significant hub of research into the nexus of politics, crime and ethnicity. Some startup funding will be required until it becomes self-sufficient in fifteen to twenty years. This is part of our think long-term strategy. Specifically, incentives should include:

$1.2 million Historical Preservation Grant

Renovation of the Glenn abandoned car barn under the Dilapidated Building Restoration Act.

Leaseback of the car barn where the local Economic Development takes title and leases it back for $1 per year so it is tax free

Funding for two positions under the Irish American Reparations Act

Creation of an institute to study How Political Crime Benefits America.

Promotion and advertising by the Michigan Department of Tourism, the State Highway Department, as well as the Pure Michigan promotional effort.

Finally, Mr. Chairman, I see where we are about out of time, so I will mention the last two very briefly. DGMG is a female-owned and -operated business needing just routine assistance.

Wave of the Future Church (WOTFC) is a faith-based project needing only modest support by our organization.

Knowing that none of you are anti-women or against religion, we will include these in the motion for approval. That concludes my report."

"Thank you, Ms. Dalrymple. That was an excellent presentation and seeing that it is about noon and time for lunch, I move we adopt the report with recommendations as outlined by the staff."

"Excuse me, excuse me, Mr. Chairman. I am Matilda Hoffenmeister, Executive Director of the Coalition of Concerned Citizens for Transparent and Ethical Government. My organization would like to know more about the DGMG and WOTFC projects before you approve government subsidies for them."

"Ms. Hoffenmeister, you are clearly out of order. Nowhere on the agenda does it allow questions from the audience. This meeting has been run according to all pertinent administrative, regulatory rules and procedures without input from special interest groups such as yours."

"Will the clerk call the roll?"

"Ms. Dancing Bear."

"Aye."

"Ms. Sanchez."

"Aye."

"Mr. Hightower."

"Aye."

Mr. Chairman, the motion is adopted."

"Ladies and gentlemen, thank you for joining us today. The commission is hereby adjourned. Let's go to lunch."

NINETEEN

Skeeter: "Bogey, did you not know that between Memorial Day and Labor Day Americans eat seven billion hot dogs?"

Bogey: "What the fuck does that have to do with anything?"

Skeeter: "I'm hungry."

Bogey and Skeeter had started their great trek north earlier that morning, fortified with only two Pop-Tarts and a 16 oz. RC Cola they had pilfered from a Quik Trip gas station. The scam was always the same. Skeeter would stand in the back of the store and scream, "Oh, my God, a copperhead," which as one of the most venomous snakes in the South would usually be enough to encourage all the customers and the clerk to beat it out the front door. Meanwhile, Bogey would have positioned himself near the single-serve Pop-Tart shelf, which in the interest of good nutrition, was usually adjacent to the soft drink dispenser, allowing him to stuff a couple of ready-to-go Pop-Tarts (Orange Crush was their favorite) into his pockets and shove a 16 oz. cola in his underwear (22 oz. was just too damn big). Sure, his gait leaving looked like someone with a pole up his ass, but who was to notice with all the excitement over the copperhead?

"Bogey, is it time to get gas yet? I can't eat another damn Pop-Tart, and now is about the time they start setting up the sampling stations at Costco. We can fill up with cheap gas, eat our way around the store at the sampling stations and fill our pockets with free food. Hell, that is why we lined the pockets of our camos with Ziplock bags. Whatever they are giving away and a couple of Bud Lights, and we are back on the road again."

Bogey: "Sounds like a plan to me. We are almost to Chattanooga, where there should be a Costco, and we can let Uncle Earl treat us to a good meal."

Bogey's Uncle Earl was now ensconced in the dementia ward of the Milledgeville State Psychiatric Hospital. During a visit, Bogey had noticed the ol' geezer's Costco card on the dresser, which he ripped off when Earl was wheeled to the afternoon community singing break. Sadly, the accompanying Visa card had been deactivated by Uncle Earl's wife, but she had not gotten around to worrying about his premium Costco membership. Replacing Earl's picture with one of Bogey wearing his Make America Great Again hat was a piece of cake.

The layout of every Costco is essentially the same, and the food sampling mix is pretty standard. Between the two of them, they had four zippered pockets — two for hard samples — e.g., cheese, crackers, nuts, etc. — and two for the main course i.e. wet samples such as Kirkland tamales and spaghetti. They bee-lined it to the food section in the back of the store where it was agreed that Bogey would fill up with the main course while Skeeter would concentrate on appetizers. A regular meal plan!

They were in luck. Since it was a Saturday, the aisles provided a virtual feast. Quick decisions had to be made as to what samples would be consumed on premise and what would be "carryout." Sometimes portability and how strict they were with "one per customer" dictated outcome.

Skeeter could not resist filling half a pocket with chocolate Twinkies and accompanied that with micro-waved andouille sausage stuffed dumplings, which he considered the perfect combo. The other pocket was dedicated to pickled asparagus and pumpkin-spiced Fiber One bites. Bogey had to consider that sauces and toppings might blend as he sloshed out the door past the receipt checker, so he was determined to combine a spicy with a mild in each zipper bag. For one pocket, he settled on Spam with buttermilk gravy and andouille sausage in a creole sauce. The other pocket came down to Kirkland Spicy Corn Dogs and Mama Mia's Ravioli. To top off the culinary delight they had assembled, and in order not to draw attention, they bought a double pack of Ritz Crackers.

After a pit stop at McDonald's where they stocked up on napkins and utensils, a roadside picnic with a six pack of Bud Lights was in order. Filled with the finest American cuisine, they were good to go again.

Battle Creek First is headquartered in what is euphemistically called downtown Battle Creek off Exit 98 on I-94 about halfway between Chicago and Detroit. Bogey and Skeeter had slept Sunday night in the truck at the rest stop at Exit 80. They clearly needed to clean up before presenting themselves Monday morning, so they headed to the Tiki Truck Stop for a deodorant bath and a change of clothes. Bogey decided to go with his favorite chartreuse colored T-shirt emblazoned in black with:

MARVINS

Your WGA Market

One Stop Shopping

Whiskey, Guns, Ammo

Skeeter opted for something more business oriented. A neon orange wife beater T-shirt inscribed:

Critter Control

Managed Road Kill

Dressed to kill, as far as they were concerned.

"Bogey, here it is. 2 W. Michigan Avenue. Looks like the office must be upstairs over the Schlotsky's Sandwich Shop."

Bounding up the narrow stairway between Schlotsky's and Monique's Massage Parlor was a directory indicating that Battle Creek First was in Room 201. Interestingly, it additionally showed that the offices of the Michigan Cannabis Development Association, Michigan Tourism

Association, Renewable Resources Coalition, WOTFC and DGMG were all located in Room 206. Rather confusing for these two Georgia good ol' boys, but they thought, What the hell.

"Hi, I'm Bogey Jackson, and this is my buddy Skeeter Williams."

"What do you want?" barked the receptionist Isabella Guenther with as much disdain as her German background could muster.

"We are here to start work under the Make West Michigan Grow Program. We talked to some Indian dude a couple of weeks ago, and he said we were to report here."

"Okay, just a minute," responded Isabella thinking God save us. "Let me get Mr. Johansson."

"Red, there are two rednecks out here, looking like something the cat dragged in, claiming they are reporting for work under the Make West Michigan Grow Program."

"What are their names?"

"This is not a joke. Bogey Jackson and Skeeter Williams."

"Okay, I will be right out."

"Well boys, welcome to West Michigan. Your timing is perfect. The legislature just approved the money for your program so I can put you on the payroll right away. The Michigan Department of Labor will be giving a grant to the Craft Brewers and the Charter Fisherman's Association to jointly administer this groundbreaking initiative and, considering the importance of this project,

I have agreed to serve as executive director. Our first organizational meeting will be tomorrow night."

"What time?"

"Ten p.m."

"Where?"

"The What Knot Inn in Glenn about an hour from here. Here is 20 bucks for a few craft beers before we meet. You may need them."

TWENTY

Rosa's appearance before Senator VanValkenberg's subcommittee had made her an overnight media sensation. Immigrant, philanthropist, religious entrepreneur all rolled into one was just beyond the pale for breathless news announcers, cable talking heads, radio and television talk show hosts. She alone with her spiritual partner, as she now referred to Armando, would be the subject of saturation media coverage by every outlet imaginable. Catholic radio dedicated a segment to the young couple entitled "Dreams and Destiny: How Faith Led Us Home." *Cubano Magazine* featured the two of them in matching guayabera shirts in what the publication called a major research piece on how the Mariel boatlift made for a better America. Even Fox News weighed in with a one-hour documentary sponsored by the immigration law firm of Garcia & Rodriguez, casting their lives as the story of how to pull yourself up by your bootstraps. The fawning over Rosa and Armando was unrelenting.

Awash in taxpayer monies and buoyed by the tsunami of media attention, Rosa and Armando were ready to launch Glenn Apothecary Gobbles and partake in the $5.4 billion cannabis industry. They renovated the old Glenn car barn using urban block grant dollars to have it take on the appearance of a turn-of-the-century pharmacy complete with a mortar and pestle on the façade and Rx in the window.

In a nod to frugality, they decided to forgo the traditional pharmacist smock and stuck with the matching Guayaberas with removable fleece linings for all-season use. In order to highlight the edible aspect of the apothecary and to keep customers totally confused, they placed a simple neon red "eat" and then *"comer"* sign above the door. The addition of the Spanish word meaning to eat, *"comer"* was a last-minute decision by Armando believing that would fulfill their commitment to Hispanic outreach.

They realized product differentiation and variety would be a key to success. The net effect was to turn the kitchen of the Airstream trailer where they lived into a virtual food factory. Usually, they would begin experimenting late at night while totally stoned and overwhelmed by the munchies after watching a couple of reruns of *Wheel of Fortune*. Being stoned allowed them to appreciate the desires of the end user and watching *Wheel* kept them in touch with the common man. The end result of this new product development process was a panoply of infused food items that would make your head spin even before digesting them. In addition to the ubiquitous cannabis cookies and cakes, they were able to create some really novel items; Munchie Chips, Laughing Girl Scout S'mores, Reefer Cola, High Times Beer, Jeb Bush Low Energy Bar, Buzz Brownies and even the Cheech and Chong Soup of the Day, all of which received the seal of approval from the Michigan Cannabis Development Association.

Trend-setting products, ideal location, taxpayer funding meant that these Ganjapreneurs were on a roll, but with one major problem. As opposed to recreational marijuana, medical marijuana requires a prescription, a concept foreign to many of their would-be customers. No prescription, no sale. Then it dawned on Armando one night while watching syndicated episodes of *Marcus Welby, MD,* on TNT, why not our own doc in a box just like Walgreens and CVS? He or she could examine the would-be customer on site and prescribe a remedy on the spot, and he knew the perfect fit for this position. Her name was Mandalay Violin. He had met her on Facebook after discovering they had a mutual friend who specialized in "nighttime immigration from Haiti to the U.S." Mandalay lived in Port-au-Prince and was a direct descendant of former dictators Papa Doc Duvalier and his son Baby Doc Duvalier. This doc lineage, combined with the fact that her father was in charge of the Tonton Macoutes was persuasive in having the Royal Haitian Academy of Medicine award her a doctor's degree after two weeks of intensive study and training. Although she spoke only Creole, Rosa was able to persuade U.S. Customs that her specialty in herb and mystic medicine was deserving of a two-year sabbatical visa to come to Michigan to share "culture experience and novel medical approaches in the clinical fields of treatment." It also didn't hurt that Rosa had threatened the Head of Customs that unless approved, she would use her newfound fame to hold a press conference attacking U.S. Customs of "systematic bias and endemic discrimination against Caribbean and people of color."

Dr. Violin entered the U.S. through Miami, whereupon, the local news station mistook her for the President of the Miami Taxi Drivers Association. When the reporter stuck a mic in her face and asked her about a threatened work action called "operation slowdown," she responded not really understanding with her limited English, "This cancer must be surgically removed," causing the Dade County tourism board to go into a frenzy at the thought of a taxi strike occurring during Gay Pride Week, and at the same time the Southern Baptist Leadership Conference was in town. It also had a ripple effect when Dr. Violin was spotted boarding a connecting flight to Chicago and Fox News came out with an Action Alert that anonymous sources indicated an effort by foreign elements to organize Chicago taxi drivers would soon be underway.

Eventually, the good doctor made her way to Glenn, where it quickly became apparent that her inability to speak English might hinder her competence in the practice of medicine. It turns out Creole was of limited use in the Snowbelt. Rosa and Armando were not to be deterred. They had a bona fide doctor with a distinguished Haitian degree, and they were going to put her to work as a doc in the box. Language was just a matter to be overcome.

The first thing they did was to develop what they called the Glenn Apothecary Comprehensive Physical Exam. Technology was to be cutting edge, so they installed a coin-operated blood pressure/heart rate machine they bought used from a defunct Rite Aid store. They also, in the name of efficiency, picked up a used change machine from a recently closed laundromat. They then devised a five-part health analysis questionnaire printed in English, Spanish and Creole. Once again providing the multilingual component as evidence of their dedication to underserved communities.

1. Your current anxiety level?
   a. More
   b. Less
   c. Same
2. Your current weight?
   a. Gained weight
   b. Lost weight
   c. Same
3. Sleep?
   a. More
   b. Less
   c. Same

4. Drugs?
   a. Heavy
   b. Light
   c. Same
5. Political affiliation?
   a. Republican
   b. Democrat
   c. None of the above

If the patient checked either a, b, or c for any of the five questions they clearly qualified for a medical marijuana prescription which Dr. Violin would then readily supply.

Business was brisk. Lines formed each morning before opening, and the mandatory blood pressure machine had become a major source of revenue, even more so with the addition of a device that, for an additional 75¢, would send the user a personalized get well email to make them feel better. Certain products became demographic favorites. Rich, white folks with second homes gravitated to Laughing Girl Scout S'mores largely due to the tie-in with National Girl Scouts of America, which was supposedly given 50¢ for each box sold to their National Drug Awareness Program. Jeb Bush Low Energy Bars tended to be the favorite of the trailer park contingent, and old hippies wearing socks with Birkenstocks seemed to enjoy the Cheech and Chong Soup of the Day. Dr. Violin had come to recognize rather quickly who fit into what category.

"My, she looks out of place," thought Dr. Violin as she spotted the woman second in line as they prepared to open Monday morning.

Tall, thin as a razor, she had the demeanor of a Doberman. Mousy-brown hair pulled back in a bun, horned-rimmed glasses, wearing a Sear's business suit with flats and carrying a copy of *The Economist*. She made Carly Fiorina look like a party girl.

"Doctor, I am in this area on a business trip and have a terrible headache. Can you prescribe me something a Dr. Violin had no idea what she was saying, so she gave her the same response she gave to everyone in broken English.

"Take blood pressure."

"I just need something for a headache," the patient replied.

"Take blood pressure."

Her head was pounding, so she decided to acquiesce to see if she could get this damn doc to write her a scrip for something heavy duty. She plopped four quarters into the machine but declined the get-well card.

Her blood pressure came in at 70-40 indicating a severe case of hypotension or, in other words a state of existence similar to a hibernating bear. Her heartbeat was 40 per minute, which put her in the range between an induced coma and a flash-frozen fish. A condition brought upon by a steady diet of Valium she had ingested over the years to address profound hyperactivity. None of the numbers really mattered since Dr. Violin had no idea what they meant anyway.

"Fill out form," instructed our doc in a box. "Doctor, all I need is a prescription for a simple pain killer. What is with this place?"

"Fill out form."

"God help us. Okay, I will fill out the damn form."

After checking "less" on the first question about anxiety, Dr. Violin grabbed the form and announced, "Exam done. Now prescription."

"What about the rest of the questionnaire?"

"Exam done. Now prescription."

Whereupon she pulled out a pre-printed form listing the products available in the Glenn Apothecary and scribbled her name on the doctor line and filled in the date.

"Your name?" she asked to complete the form.

"What the hell kind of drugstore is this!"

"Your name?"

"Shit — Matilda Hoffenmeister."

TWENTY-ONE

Berdenna realized it would be problematic for her to be front and center at the incentive meeting between the Michigan Economic Development Committee (MEDC) and DGMG Inc. Those bothersome open meeting laws with all that nonsense about transparency meant that it would be public information and available to all those meddlesome reporters as to who attended and who was wallowing in the public trough. Once her name surfaced, someone was bound to make the connection with her husband the senator and impugn the integrity of the entire transaction. It was best to keep her role under wraps and put demented second cousin Audrey front and center.

Garden of Peace Rest Home in Holland, Michigan, was affectionately known as "Creeper Village," due in part to the large number of residents moving about with walkers. Audrey Richenberg, at age 94, had been a resident of the psych ward for 10 years, having been diagnosed with severe dissociative identify disorder. Manifestations of the malady resulted in her believing she was Marilyn Monroe incarnated. Her days were spent repeatedly watching the movie *Gentlemen Prefer Blondes* dressed in a long, slinky dress mimicking Marilyn's attire and singing varying renditions of "Diamonds Are a Girl's Best Friend." Most of the men in the ward considered themselves current Joe DiMaggio and therefore entitled to all that "Marilyn" had to offer, making nap time a period of robust entertainment.

As Berdenna wheeled up to the Garden of Peace, she knew handling Audrey would be tricky but crucial if she was to get the incentive package without the Van-Valkenberg name surfacing. Any footprints to her husband's role could ruin the deal. She had scheduled the meeting with the MEDC as one between the commission and Ms. Audrey Richenberg, CEO of DGMG Inc.

Always punctual, Audrey was sitting on the welcome bench outside when Berdenna pulled up. Having been told that "Marilyn" was needed in a role, she was in full Marilyn Monroe regalia. Low-slung blouse, miniskirt, facial beauty mark, glistening red lipstick and a muskrat stole wrapped around her neck. Ready for show time.

"Hello, Marilyn, hop in. We are off to a big meeting where you have a major role to play," chirped Berdenna to Audrey as she opened the passenger door and presented herself as Marilyn's agent.

"Darling, to what studio are we headed?" responded Audrey in her best Marilyn breathless intonation.

"Actually, we are headed to the state capitol for a shoot, and you play the part of Audrey Richenberg,

CEO of DGMG Inc. in a meeting with high government officials. You don't need to say much. Just be the coy corporate executive periodically making listening noises like "fine," "interesting," and "strategic."

"How about singing and dancing, and who is my leading man?"

"Please, Marilyn, no singing or dancing. Remember this part calls for you to be a staid businesswoman. Your name is Audrey Richenberg, a conservative, German, taciturn CEO type."

"What about the leading man?"

"Chairing the meeting will be an elderly fellow named Jack Hightower, who is the leading man of the Michigan Economic Development Commission. He will read off a list of incentives they plan to award DGMG and then ask you to sign some documents agreeing to the terms. Remember, no singing or dancing, just listening noises. If you pull this off as Audrey Richenberg, you will be up for an Oscar and another square in front of Grauman's Chinese Theatre. This is big."

It was a gray, dull day in Lansing, which matched the dull-gray government building that housed the MEDC. Berdenna and Audrey strolled down the long corridor to Conference Room A, which was posted as the location for the meeting. Berdenna had decided, if asked who she was, to explain that she was merely Ms. Richenberg's caregiver and as such under federal HIPAA regulations was not allowed to divulge her name or her company.

Opening the door, Audrey entered with hips gyrating to such an extent that it looked like she was moving sideways — what they used to describe as Marilyn's "horizontal walk." Twirling her muskrat stole, she exclaimed with smoky sincerity, "Gentlemen," looking directly at Chairman Hightower, "it is so good to be here. Hopefully, we can work together and develop a meaningful relationship, if you know what I mean."

Jack Hightower was so excited by this entrance; Viagra wasn't even required. A sporty fellow at 92, he thought of himself as the gray fox ever since his wife had left him five years earlier for a retired accordion player from *The Lawrence Welk Show.* Jack was convinced he had a lot of seeds to sow, and the entrance of Ms. Richenberg had put him into a palpating frenzy.

"Well, welcome, Ms. Richenberg," he nervously blurted out while almost being overcome by the lust in his heart.

Grabbing his cane, he ambled over to her, grasping her hand with both of his.

"On behalf of the MEDC, I see a new relationship developing with great potential. May I ask who that is accompanying you?"

"I am Ms. Richenberg's caregiver and under federal HIPAA regulations, I am unable to provide my name or the name of the company. Privacy reasons and all that."

"I understand," replied Chairman Hightower. "We sure don't want to break any federal laws. You sure look familiar."

"Happens all the time. People mistake me for Rosie the Riveter without the bandanna."

"That makes sense to me," responded Chairman Hightower. "Ms. Richenberg, why don't you sit here next to me so I can look down — I mean, check out — I mean describe the benefits I can bestow on DGMG."

"Ooh, thank you, Mr. Chairman," purred Audrey.

"Ms. Richenberg, for the record, can you briefly describe the nature of DGMG's business?"

"Yes, darling, it is quite simple. It is all about customer satisfaction delivered on a personal basis with years of experience. We plan to offer an array of beverages served in a unique stimulating fashion. Why, after one stop at our shop, you may not need that cane anymore."

At this point, with Jack's imagination running wild, Audrey began rubbing her foot up and down his calf under the table causing him to enter a state of extreme hyperventilation. Seeing him in a near convulsive state, the recording secretary yanked the emergency defibrillator off the wall and threw him to the ground administering shock treatment. Meanwhile, Audrey hopped onto the conference table and broke out into her favorite rendition of" Diamonds Are a Girl's Best Friend," all the while swinging her muskrat stole over the horizontal convulsing chairman, exacerbating his manic state. Finally, some semblance of order was restored when three rent-a-cops stormed the room, catapulting Audrey off the table with a Taser while Chairman Hightower continued to unconsciously convulse on the floor.

In the midst of all this chaos, Berdenna forged Audrey's signature on the agreement documents and stamped approved in the commission's decision block. The agreement was quite generous, but not surprising since it had been drafted by Senator VanValkenberg's two new interns. It called for DGMG to receive:

A $450,000 grant from the state Female Venture Capital Fund

Expedited restaurant licensing

Exemption from all sanitation and health licensing requirements

A 99-year lease at $1 per year for use of the old Glenn Post Office Building

Infrastructure improvements including the creation of two drive-through lanes

Finally, something quite unusual: designation of the Glenn site as an enhanced First Amendment/Freedom of Expression zone for the Visual Arts.

Medics quickly arrived to cart off the comatose chairman. Berdenna flashed the senator's wife ID card to one of the rent-a-cops and with the hint of a possible promotion, convinced him to toss unconscious Audrey over his shoulder and deposit her in the car.

On the drive back, the totally disheveled Audrey finally came to.

"How did the shoot go?"

"You were terrific. In fact, it went so well, you may have to perform that role again in a couple of weeks."

"I play Audrey again?"

"Yes"

"Where?"

"Glenn"

TWENTY-TWO

E conomic development officials, politicians and company brass all love groundbreaking ceremonies for the same and also somewhat dissimilar reasons. First and foremost, they get attention, which feeds the insatiable egos they all possess. These events also have a mercenary application. Economic development types use the ceremony as a means to validate how effective their organization is by claiming that hundreds if not thousands of jobs will be created as a result of all their hard work, even though the number and quality announced rarely ever comes to fruition. Politicians being politicians, they love the limelight and the opportunity to take credit for something that they usually had little if anything to do with. Businesses, not government, creates jobs, is the usual conservative mantra — except when there is a ribbon cutting/groundbreaking during which business and government can take credit for creating jobs. Finally, those corporate types who distain government relish being fawned over in the spotlight, providing a perfect photo op in the same annual report in which they blame government regulation and over-reach as the reason they did not quite make the numbers.

The arrival of ERR LLC in West Michigan warranted a full-scale media feast with all the self-congratulatory, back-slapping, pomp and circumstance the parties could muster. Red wanted the whole affair to be first class and was ready to pull out all the stops to make it happen. A white tent was erected over the fracking pipe, which had been painted green to connote a symbiotic relationship between the project and nature. American flags were placed at each corner to stir the patriotic juices of all in attendance, and a banner was strewn across the front proudly proclaiming America Energy Free at Last. So what if the energy coming out of that pipe wouldn't be enough to run a Yugo for a day. This endeavor was aspirational! Rows of white folding chairs were lined in front with a red carpet down the middle. Guests would be met by Boy Scouts working to attain their Stewards of the Environment badges, and the national anthem would be sung by the 8th grade stepdaughter of the chair of the Michigan Department of Environmental Quality. Following the ceremony, light refreshments would be served at the Community Center manned by the last three surviving members of the local WWII Veterans Club.

It takes about two and half hours for the ERR LLC Falcon 900 to fly from Texas to South Haven, Michigan. On board this fall morning was Boone Cartwright, Brooke Blackstone, Montavious Sharp and Ron White. Boone was

abnormally uptight about this event. The corporate headquarters back in Houston had been the daily scene of
demonstrations by former Bernie Sanders supporters pil-
laging the company as a "criminal enterprise savaging our
air and water," while "concentrating wealth in the hands of
the few." Exacerbating the situation, they were joined just
yesterday by the Rev. Jesse Jackson, who demanded that
the Falcon jet be turned over to his Rainbow Coalition
where it could be put to use by those who "suffer servitude
under corporate oppressors." Actually, Boone did not give
a shit what Jesse or the demonstrators did or said, but he
was concerned that the ongoing attention might cause the
media to delve deeper into what his company did and did
not do.

"Montavious," come on up here and tell me how we
have orchestrated this event," barked Boone.

Boone was sitting up front in the plane wearing his
usual cowboy oil man shtick of bolo tie, rodeo belt buckle,
boots and a Stetson. Sitting across from him was Brooke in
a Michael Kors miniskirt, Jimmy Choo sleeveless see-
through blouse and 4 inch Manolo Blahnik heels completed
with a glistening diamond aligned perfectly in her cleavage.
Needless to say, she had the chairman's attention.

"Montavious it is critical that we have the right mix
of would-be employees in attendance to demonstrate
our cultural sensitivity. Also, Ron has informed me that
designation as a Disadvantaged Business Enterprise (DBE)
will help keep state and federal tax examiners away since

the media will posture us as a politically correct company. Most important, DBE designation provides double-tax credit, and it can only be attained through the right mix of employees. Isn't that right, Ron?"

"Yes, sir," blurted Ron from the back row of the plane.

"I think you will be quite happy with the amalgamation of individuals and causes I have been able to recruit," responded Montavious. First, I have instructed that no one is to be referred to as he or she, but rather ze. By using genderless pronouns, we will create a non-threatening communal atmosphere. Participating with us in the audience will be six same-gender loving individuals, seven citizens of advanced age, two of which use walkers, three are in wheelchairs, one is the regional rep for AARP and the other is a field organizer for the Gray Panthers. We also have three attendees who have been declared non-binary, two indigenous Americans and a non-disabled white guy with his niece who is a Girl Scout hoping to become a social worker after a stint in the Peace Corps. Finally, for the sake of authenticity, I have hired a laid-off professional pickets, at minimum wage, from the AFL-CIO to man a burn barrel and carry a placard proclaiming, 'The end is near. Come to Jesus and repent or burn in hell for eternity.'"

"Montavious, hiring the demonstrators is brilliant. That will draw the attention off the press and keep us from being asked any detailed questions. What do you think Ron?"

"I agree!"

"Brooke?"

"Tactical."

"Who else will be coming that I need to know about?"

"Well, sir, there is quite a list of local business leaders and community activists, but attendees of note include Governor Baumgarten; Senator VanValkenberg with his wife Berdenna; his two staffers Sean O'Malley and Paddy Fitzpatrick; Jack Hightower, who is the Chair of the Michigan Economic Development Commission and, of course, Red Johansson, who you know, head of Battle Creek First, and his wife Ingrid."

"What about the actual event? How long will it last? Who is speaking, and do I have prepared remarks?"

"The actual ceremony should only last about 15 minutes, followed by 5 minutes or so for photos and then you need to make a cameo appearance for let's say 10 minutes at the community gathering where you pretend like you really give a damn about what they feel or think. After that torture, it is wheels up and we are on our way back to Texas.

"As far as speaking, Red of Battle Creek First will act as MC welcoming you and the other distinguished guests. Governor Baumgarten will then speak, and I am sure bloviate ad nauseam about how his pro-business policies have created the conditions for economic growth and full employment making this announcement possible. The only saving grace will be if he understands food is being served afterwards, he may cut it short.

"Next is your turn and I have prepared a couple of pages of the usual indecipherable corporate speak. You will mention our mission, shared values, culture, outreach to communities of different colors, nationalities, religion, sexual orientation and political persuasion. You finish by extolling the ol' public/private partnership bit, which translates into "Thanks for the money." You then introduce Senator VanValkenberg.

"The good senator will drone on about Christian values and the work ethic being the linchpin of this region while thanking God, the taxpayers and the MEDC for making all of this possible. The length of his remarks will be dictated by the size of the crowd and whether he thinks anyone from the Christian Coalition might be in attendance.

"Finally, it will be the turn of Jack Hightower of the MEDC, who may take a while to get to the mic depending on whether his walker gets stuck in a rut. He will announce that today is actually a christening of the pipe rather than a groundbreaking and that the Rev. Odacious Jackson of the Calvary Baptist Church will lead us in prayer. By the way, we are thanking the reverend for his spiritual participation by giving him use of the plane this winter to fly him and a 25-year old female parishioner needing spiritual guidance to Bimini for a week. It was the least we could do."

"This sounds great. What do you think, Ron?"

"Couldn't agree more."

"Brooke?"

"Strategic."

"One last thing, Montavious. Is there anything of concern that might require a heads up?"

"No, not really. Someone said the executive director of the Coalition of Concerned Citizens for Transparent and Ethical Government was seen snooping around town the other day, but I can't imagine what she could do to spoil the festivities. I think we have everything under control."

TWENTY-THREE

The gig as interns with Senator VanValkenberg was just about as good as it could get for a couple of rummies from the Southside of Chicago. Paddy and Sean didn't do shit. They were on the Senate payroll but did little, if anything, for the district they ostensibly worked for. Their primary responsibility was tending to the personal needs of the senator and his princess wife Berdenna. Picking up the dry cleaning, taking her to yoga and the all-important role as state paid Uber drivers each evening as Senator VanValkenberg and the Mrs. went from one lobbyist reception to another enjoying the free food and booze. Paddy and Sean were not simply passive observers of these events but rather active participants relishing their roles as 'legislative staff,' imbibing at will and hitting on everything in a skirt. What a life. Getting paid to do essentially nothing, tooling around town party to party acting like big shots all the while in the relentless pursuit of poontang.

"Hey guys, come on in. I need to talk with you," barked Senator VanValkenberg as he entered the Senate office.

The Irish duo looked at each other in concern. This did not sound good. They usually spent mornings creating vacuous certificates of recognition for constituents. Meaningless pieces of paper carrying the Senate seal to give an aura of authenticity to something that was simply a political sop to mundane groups and businesses, e.g.

Certificate of Recognition to the Conservation Club of Otsego for supporting the Black Swallowtail as the state butterfly.

Certificate of Recognition to the Road Kill Diner for creative culinary development.

Certificate of Recognition to Fennville Auto Repair for going one month without a consumer complaint.

It was an endless process pumping these out on behalf of Senator VanValkenberg. If they ran out of constituents to be "recognized," they would simply pull out the Yellow Pages and take it from there.

"Well, fellas, take a seat. I think it is time we take a look at your futures and where we as a team go from here." Senator VanValkenberg instructed Sean and Paddy, motioning them to sit on the couch across from his desk.

The two of them took a seat nervously glancing at each other. Any time he used the "team" bullshit and "we" in the same sentence, whatever was coming down was not good for anybody other than the senator.

"Gentlemen, my term in office will be ending soon and with it your staff positions. That being said, I know you share my dedication to public service, and I would like to entertain a new role I have envisioned for you.

"As you may recall, in the last economic development bill, I reported out of the subcommittee, there was funding for the creation of a National Political Corruption Hall of Fame under the code name Project Jailbird. This provision allows for two positions to be funded under the Irish Americans Reparations Act in recognition of the oppression suffered by the Irish here in America since the potato famine. The confluence of this new Hall of Fame and how it is to be staffed prompted me to undertake a national search last night on my iPad for co-directors. After almost an hour searching the website of the Ancient Order of Hibernians, I came to the conclusion that no duo is more qualified to assume these positions as co-directors than the two of you. Extensive backgrounds in criminal justice and political science coupled with your deep cultural roots and knowledge of the plight of Irish Americans makes you eminently positioned to assume these critical posts."

"What the fuck is he talking about?" the two of them wondered. What did catch their attention was when he referenced "public service," which was code for being on the government payroll in some form or fashion. That was always good. So what if they knew nothing about running a hall of fame? They had learned a lot about political corruption when they went to work at the state capitol each day. As far as the Irish bit, well, hell, they had been in every bar called Dubliner, Shamrock or the like within a 500-mile radius.

"Thank you, senator," responded Sean. "I speak for both of us when I tell you how honored and appreciative we are of your endorsement for these positions. We realize they require a certain gravitas, which can only be acquired through experience and education. Commitment, character and judgment are attributes that are critical to the success of the mission. In light of these and upon sober reflection, hell, yes, we want the jobs. How much do they pay?"

"Well, gentlemen, that is good news. I thought you might be interested in these positions. As far as compensation and staffing are concerned, you will be using state funds so parsimony and frugality will be the order of the day. I suggest you use the Clinton Foundation and the Trump Foundation as organizations to emulate so as to avoid charges of excessive compensation, self-dealing or political cronyism. In this regard, let me be emphatic that I want no role to play, but if I could help as a consultant to say at the tune of $250,000 per year, I would be glad to entertain such a notion in the spirit of giving back what the good Lord has given me."

"Senator, it would be an honor to have you associated with this undertaking. Your insight and experiences would be invaluable in creating a National Political Corruption Hall of Fame. No substitute for first-hand knowledge."

"This is great guys. We now need to tend to the people's business. There is a ribbon cutting in Glenn today organized by Battle Creek First, which I need to attend, and Berdenna is going with me. Why don't the two of you come? And since it is official business, you can get the state to reimburse you for your mileage. Most important, you can check out the proposed site of the Hall of Fame and meet some of the locals. Plus, there is a free buffet afterwards."

"We're on it, boss."

TWENTY-FOUR

S keeter and Bogey were very good at doing nothing. Especially when nothing involved sitting in a bar with a few bucks in their pockets. It was now about midnight and they had been bellied up to the bar at The What Knot Inn waiting for Red since about 5 p.m. This was to be the first meeting with him to kick off their new jobs, but it was clear he was a no show. Things looked so bleak that Bogey kept punching in on the jukebox that country classic, "If The Phone Don't Ring, You'll Know It's Me."

Skeeter: "Bogey, did you not know that the world record for people at one time dancing in wooden shoes is 2,605?"

Bogey: "You are a complete asshole. We have driven over a 1,000 miles to this frozen tundra for jobs only to get stiffed by that bastard in Battle Creek. Why would you bring up some bullshit about wooden shoes?"

"Come on, man, we are only 15 miles from Holland where there are a bunch of Dutch people running around, so I thought it might be important to know."

Well, what is important is that we find that sorry ass Red Johansson and make him deliver on all those promises he made or else we are going to look like a couple of sorry fools when we return to Hahira with our tails between our legs."

It was about this time when last call was announced, and Bogey staggered back to the john for one last pit stop before another night in the truck. Standing at the urinal with a mind addled by a dozen or so Bud Lights, he tried to focus on a poster inviting all to some community event at the old Glenn Golf Course. The more he tried to focus, the more he squinted and the more he began to sway back and forth, causing him to mightily miss his urinary target. The floor was becoming a slippery mess as his beer-soaked brain finally began to comprehend what he was reading; his swaying became violent with agitation. Something had to give.

"God damn it, I feel like shit. Where are we?" moaned Bogey.

"In the truck, you idiot. We're in the parking lot of The What Knot Inn. After you passed out on the john floor, the bouncer and I carted you out with a dolly and tossed you in here. The only way we knew something had happened to you was a woman in the adjoining bathroom heard you yell, 'That bastard is coming to town,' followed by a loud thud which must have been you hitting the floor. She yelled, 'Sweet Jesus, he must be dead,' at which we barged in to find you comatose on the floor holding your pecker, which was standing at half-mast. Not a pretty sight."

"Well, no wonder I feel like hell, but as you tell me what happened, I am beginning to remember what I saw. That SOB Red Johansson is going to be here in Glenn later today at some kind of ceremony. I can't remember the details, but if we go back into The What Knot Inn over the pisser, there is a poster telling all about it. We need to show up there and beat the shit out of him for stiffing us last night."

Governor Baumgarten was never one to miss a groundbreaking or ribbon cutting, and the event in Glenn was no exception. His whole career had been built on taking credit where none was due and deflecting responsibility when something went wrong. As governor, he had taken both of these traits to new shameless heights. He also was a master at positioning himself between a TV camera and the focal point of the event where he would make some inane comments about public-private partnership, synergies and positioning the state for growth. He would then waddle over to the buffet table where, with years of experience, he could balance a full plate, a beverage, a fork and consume it all while standing in line for seconds. The only time he would take off his feed bag was when something in a skirt would approach necessitating he take out his handkerchief to wipe off the sweat of lust from his forehead. An occurrence that was becoming more routine, ever since his wife, who was a yoga instructor and advocate of holistic health, left him in disgust for a guru of a vegan diet after the governor told her his dream job was becoming a board member of Dunkin' Donuts. Unbridled of any pretense of marital duty, his mind was in a continuous state of carnal capitulation.

Now approaching the end of his second and final term, with no political path forward, he was especially looking forward to the event in Glenn as a means to further ingratiate himself with the oil industry. Already a favorite after he was quoted as saying, "What is the big deal about a little earthquake?" when challenged by environmentalist for signing legislation making Michigan a sanctuary state for fracking. The idea of getting to meet the delegation from ERR LLC presented the opportunity to see what he might do before leaving office with an eye toward some lucrative position with them after government service.

Red was pumped. The deal with ERR LLC was finally coming to fruition and, more important, so was the creation of the Wave of the Future Church and the bounty it would provide. After all those years of putting up with those pompous corporate types, he was about to get his fair share. WOTFC, under the tutelage of Ingrid as a universal life minister, would have access to all "water and mineral rights" with Lake Michigan only a half mile away. All of the attention in Glenn would be on ERR LLC and the dignitaries assembled to celebrate restoration fracking, creating new jobs and visions of economic vitality. The quaint notion of a new church simultaneously being established will be of little notice to anyone other than a few Bible thumpers and the local chapter of the Christian Coalition.

"Ingrid, are you about ready to go? We can't be late for this event," barked Red to her upstairs.

"Almost, I'm having trouble with this tab collar, and I am not sure whether this pink shirt goes with this fuchsia robe. Also, this miter might be a little bit much."

"Where did you get all this liturgical garb?"

"It was a package deal on the Discount Clergy Apparel website, which was a cross-link with the Universal Life Minister website. I even got a 10% discount."

"Well, if it was sold as a package, it must match, so let's go with it."

Rosa and Armando decided to close early. Seemed like everyone was going to the shindig at the old golf course, so why stay open? Plus, it was a way to see their benefactors at Battle Creek First, the people who had put them in business without a nickel of their own money.

Business had been booming. They had so many repeat customers, they had to install a Xerox machine so that all Dr. Violin had to do was run a copy of the previous prescription and just put in a new date. This expedited process kept the lines to a minimum, especially when any type of rock concert was in the vicinity. The nearby Glenn Store was a direct beneficiary of their success. An economic ripple effect cited by Battle Creek First and

Lansing as proof of the positive impact of economic incentives. The store was deluged by customers looking for Twinkies and Hostess Cupcakes, requiring them to eliminate the entire line of Weight Watchers products and Lean Cuisine to make more shelf space. In addition, The What Knot Inn had such a huge spike in requests to play "In-A-Gadda-Da-Vida" by Iron Butterfly, they just put it on continuous repeat.

Finally, in the unanticipated consequences category, the success of the apothecary even had an impact on traffic, whereas before cars used to speed through Glenn with barely a glance, now drivers, post-prescription, would barely exceed 5 mph. The change was so dramatic that AAA actually gave the store an award for road rage containment. The impact on customers was so universal, they could only remember one exception, and it was that razor thin woman this morning. Despite having her prescription filled, she had left totally unhinged. Top down on her Subaru convertible, laughing and popping Girl Scout S'mores, she burned some rubber as she peeled out with 'White Rabbit' by Jefferson Airplane blasting and her screaming, "This ain't the pill mother used to give me!"

TWENTY-FIVE

I t was a Chamber of Commerce day on steroids. Puffy, white clouds, temp in the sixties, leaves gold and red. This was a perfect fall day for the ERR LLC launch and a new house of worship for the God-fearing souls of Glenn. Quite a gala.

It was only 9 a.m., but a few early birds were already arriving for the 10 a.m. ceremony. They were mostly blue hairs and their husbands with walkers, who regarded this as the highlight of the week and were anxious not to miss out on the gift bags. A huge welcome banner emblazoned with the Battle Creek First logo strung across the highway as a greeting to participants coming from either direction. The paid demonstrator with his burn barrels was positioned directly across from the main entrance with a placard that read, "The End is Near: Repent." Boy Scouts served as parking attendants waving cars into an adjacent field where they were directed into neat rows. The South Haven High School marching band provided the musical backdrop altering between renditions of "Onward Christian Soldiers" and "Take the Money and Run," by The Steve Miller Band.

Once parked, guests were escorted by members of the VFW Outpost 22 along a balloon-lined pathway to a cordoned off area with another banner proclaiming "Christians for Energy Independence." The reception area was provided courtesy of the Glenn Area Fitness Council and had available coffee, Tang, doughnut holes, Pop-Tarts and weenies wrapped in dough (pigs in a blanket from Walmart). In addition, everyone was given a swag bag containing his-and-her T-shirts inscribed with "Glenn: What a Fracking Place" on the front, a Saint Christopher dashboard statue for the car from the Wave of the Future Church, a beer mug from The What Knot Inn with "One for the Road Is Never Too Many" motto, a coupon from the Glenn Apothecary for a free physical and another coupon announcing a soon-to-be-open drive-through coffee shop that will have a one-time double BOGO event the first day — details to follow.

The caterers were still setting up when Red and Ingrid were the first to arrive. It was agreed that Ingrid, as part of the ceremony, would bless the pipe, so she had bought a used aspergillum from the defrocked priest on her board to sprinkle the holy water. Having a miter on her head, clerical garb and an official holy water dispensing device in her hand made her look like something right out of the Vatican.

Armando and Rose arrived shortly after Red and Ingrid, wearing fleece-lined Guayaberas and reeking of marijuana. They had sat in the car with the windows up to smoke a few joints and benefit from the positive impact of second-hand smoke. In a slow-motion gait, they headed directly to the doughnut holes in an attempt to satisfy an overwhelming attack of the munchies.

Following the two druggists came the VanValkenberg contingent, composed of the senator, his wife Berdenna and the two loyal staffers, Sean and Paddy. As usual, Senator VanValkenberg was a glad-handing machine. Sort of a modern-day Hubert Humphrey — gab and all. He would work a crowd for hours, and getting him from the car to the reception area was a lengthy process. He had to shake the hand and yell, "Hey, friend" to everyone in sight. Berdenna seemed to have taken on a new persona for the occasion. Instead of her usual dour matronly attire, she looked like she had taken a page from the COYOTE manual. Four-inch F-me pumps, a miniskirt that looked like it had been spray painted on and her bountiful rack on full display. She seemed to attract a mostly male crowd, and to each she would hand a frequent purchaser card for the soon-to-be-opened Glenn Coffee Shop which she exclaimed would be the most stimulating place they could imagine. Ten stamps on the card would entitle the bearer to enjoy the pleasure of what would soon be a world-renowned double BOGO. Trailing behind and completely lost in the shuffle came Sean and Paddy. They could hardly see straight;

they were so hung over. Their objective was to get to the reception area and pound down Chocolate Mocha Pop-Tarts in the hope that an extreme sugar high coupled with the mocha caffeine would alleviate some of their pain until a pub opened.

Next came Chairman Jack Hightower hobbling down the lane with his cane. He had not seen or heard from Ms. Audrey Richenberg since the tumultuous last meeting of the MEDC in Lansing. Anticipating she might be in attendance, he had prepared by popping two Cialis pills on the drive down assured by the bathtub commercials that he would have 36 hours to make his move. Luckily the weather was cool enough to justify an overcoat, which would mask his excitement should he become prematurely aroused. An event that did occur when he was greeted by Berdenna VanValkenberg resulting in his pill-assisted blood pressure shooting above 160 and having him request a seat from the Boy Scouts so he could "catch his breath."

Mingling and small talk were well underway when Red noticed two grimacing fellows standing behind the last row of chairs. One was wearing a Make America Great Again cap and a chartreuse T-shirt emblazoned with MARVINS — Your WGA Market — One Stop Shopping — Whiskey, Guns, Ammo. The other had head gear that proclaimed Security by Smith & Wesson and a neon orange T-shirt promoting Critter Control — Managed Road Kill. Neither looked very happy. Doing a double take, he realized it was Bogey and Skeeter. Holy shit, with all the hoopla and excitement over today's announcement, he had forgotten he was supposed to meet them last night. This was not good. They looked totally torqued off. Somehow, after the event, he would have to beat it out the back to avoid their wrath. Not sure how, but he would figure it out on the fly.

Thank God for a distraction — here comes Governor Baumgarten.

Experienced Lansing hands knew never to impede the governor when he was focused on the food line. He would feign interest in anyone who approached but would inevitably keep plodding ahead until he had some Tang and a weenie in a blanket in hand. Today was no different. He would stay encamped at the food service section happy as a pig in slop until called to duty.

Finally, up came the requisite stretch-black limo with the gang from Texas. First out was Boone with his customary cowboy/oilman outfit of boots, bolo tie and Stetson. Next came Brooke in a pair of fur-lined high heel Uggs, Louis Vuitton sunglasses, Bebe lace mini dress and a Victoria's Secret cold shoulder wrap top. Following Brooke was Montavious in a pin-striped Hart Schaffner Marx suit, Gucci tie, Jimmy Choo loafers and a Burberry raincoat. Trailing behind was Ron in a Men's Wearhouse suit, Sear's tie and scruffy brown shoes, toting a briefcase from Staples. All persons accounted for.

"Ladies and gentlemen, my name is Jack Hightower, the chairman of the Michigan Economic Development

Commission. We welcome you to this august occasion. Please take your seats, and we will begin the formal program."

Red was keeping a wary eye on Bogey and Skeeter. One had a police baton attached to his belt and the other what looked like brass knuckles, which he would repeatedly ball into a fist inside the other hand. Interestingly, they kept standing behind the back row as others took their seats.

"Thank you, everyone. We are now ready to begin the program. First, let me introduce the dignitaries seated behind me on the dais. On my left, your right, we have Mr. Red Johansson, President of Battle Creek First, and next to him is his wife, the Reverend Ingrid Johansson, who will convey a special blessing. On my right, your left, is the Honorable Jaap VanValkenberg, our state senator, and next to him, his voluptuous, I'm sorry I meant lovely, wife Berdenna who will be making a special announcement of her own later this month. Seated next to her is someone we all know and admire, the governor of our great state, Earl Baumgarten. And finally our distinguished and special guest, Boone Cartwright, chairman and CEO of ERR LLC. Welcome to you all. I now would like to ask Red Johansson whose hard work and dedication made all this possible, to please join me at the mic."

"Thanks, Jack — this is a historic occasion for Glenn and West Michigan as we welcome the re-entry into this region of a proud industry through one of the great companies in the United States. None of this would have been possible, however, were it not for the commitment and tenacity of our esteemed State Senator Jaap VanValkenberg. Jaap, please come join me."

"Thank you, Red, and distinguished guests. I share with you the excitement of this event and what it means to our community. Here on the shores of Lake Michigan, some naysayers claim oil and water don't mix, but we are here to prove them wrong. They are the effete snobs who prattle on about climate change. Well, we are here to show them we mean business in West Michigan! It is now my distinct honor to introduce our get things done Governor Earl Baumgarten."

"Thank you, Jaap. As the governor of this great state, there is nothing I enjoy more than welcoming new business, especially one with a national reputation such as ERR LLC. Their presence here today is proof that we are open for business. World renowned for their ethics, diversity and commitment to the environment, ERR is the grand prize for economic developers. A prize we have earned today, but with no further ado, let me present to you Boone Cartwright, chairman and CEO of our newest corporate citizen."

"Thank you, governor. I can't tell you how happy we are to be here today. We look at this as another opportunity for environmental restoration. Money has always been secondary to our mission, which is focused on healing the environment. We believe in a higher purpose and therefore, instead of a ribbon cutting or groundbreaking, we have asked our new neighbor the Reverend Ingrid

GEORGE FRANKLIN

Johansson of the Wave of the Future Church if she would grace us with a blessing."

At this cue, the group on the dais came down the side step and gathered around the rusted pipe sticking out of the ground, which was dripping black goo into a Jiffy Lube recycling canister. The dripping was made possible by the ingenuity of placing a Home Depot plant self-watering device underground in a bucket of used oil. Photos of this would come in handy should the IRS ever challenge whether the company ever did recover oil.

Ingrid in all her spiritual splendor was sprinkling holy water onto the pipe with the aspergillum, invoking the blessings of Jesus and interspersing biblical quotes with a word or two of Latin. The whole scene was so captivating that no one seemed to notice the light blue convertible Subaru careening toward the site.

Matilda had left the apothecary on a mission to restore transparency to government by exposing self-dealings and insider enrichment such as was taking place at the old Glenn Golf Course. Her group, The Coalition of Concerned Citizens for Transparency and Ethical Government, had sources on the staff of the legislature, which leaked to her the connection of WOTFC and DGMG to Red Johansson and Senator Jaap VanValkenberg. Her trip to Glenn was intended as an opportunity to confront the co-conspirators at the public gathering and with media present. The problem was that she and the car were out of control. After leaving the apothecary, she decided to try her prescription of Laughing Girl Scout S'mores and proceeded to consume triple the usual amount recommended resulting in her quite simply becoming completely stoned out of her mind. A state of mental disarray reigniting in her a latent lust for the governor.

Unbeknownst to anyone, she and the governor had had a little tryst a few months earlier after a Save the Whales conference. Sure, Governor Baumgarten was an environmental Luddite, but for some reason he felt an affinity for whales and decided to attend after he learned shrimp scampi was being served. Matilda was a panelist, and in an effort to convert him to the cause and also authenticate the old adage politics makes strange bedfellows, she suggested the two of them take a field trip to Myrtle Beach, South Carolina, to go whale watching. Although they never left the room at The Buccaneer Resort, both parties considered the trip a success and for reasons of political preservation agreed to keep quiet about the action-packed weekend.

The Girl Scout S'mores had aroused in her an uncontrollable carnal desire for the rotund governor. In order to whet his appetite while driving to the event, she decided to take a topless selfie which she would Snapchat to him. Convertible top down, she ripped off her sweater, which flew out the back and began grappling with her bra with both hands while steering with her knees. She then placed her phone on the dashboard while putting her seat in full recline mode to give the honorable governor a panoramic view. The trouble with the seat adjustment was that it inadvertently caused her to push on the gas pedal, resulting in a topless car and driver careening down the road exceeding 90 mph while successfully snapping and sending a picture.

Governor Baumgarten was gathered with the others around the ground pipe listening to the Reverend Ingrid drone on when he realized a new Snapchat had arrived. Surreptitiously pulling his phone out and holding it down the side of his leg, he glanced down to see a topless shot of Matilda in a reclining position, hair blowing in the wind, tongue out and middle finger extended. The photo had the intended effect. He broke out into a cold sweat and his knees began to buckle. Just an Ingrid was extolling the importance of sharing the bounty of the land, the governor teetered forward executing a complete frontal face plant on the table holding the holy water. The audience broke out into murmurs of concern, which were quickly replaced by screams of terror at the sight of a convertible Subaru barreling down at full speed, out of control, at the gathering on the old golf course completely.

TWENTY-SIX

What a gift during the rating season for a station with the motto, "If it bleeds it leads." Channel 2 Action News was all over this breaking event with a banner alert in red proclaiming, "Carnage in Glenn." The Skycam helicopter had been dispatched to provide Eye in the Sky exclusive footage and a team of breathless reporters dispatched to give in-depth analysis. Hell, this was better than a mass murder!

Turns out a light blue convertible Subaru, for some unknown reason, had at breaking speeds veered off the highway, traversed into a drainage ditch, crossed an abandoned golf course and proceeded to plow full steam into a crowd of dignitaries and citizens gathered to celebrate a new business coming to the community. The esteemed group included the governor, a state senator and his wife, local economic development officials as well as the CEO of a company and some of his lieutenants. The scene was one of total chaos, being aptly described by one lonely protestor as the civic equivalent of a grease fire in a restaurant kitchen. Although it was still undetermined as to the extent of the injuries, Channel 2 was quickly joined in the coverage by national cable networks. Fox News, citing unnamed sources, warned ominously of a possible terrorist attack in Glenn where a Muslim had been spotted only a few weeks earlier. CNN began to publicize "Heroes in the Heartland" based on reports that the extent of the injuries would have been much greater had it not been for the actions of two unknown individuals, one described as wearing a Critter Control shirt and the other an ad for Your WGA Market.

Bogey and Skeeter had catapulted into the national limelight. Standing in the very back as the ceremony began, they were the first to encounter the renegade auto. Skeeter turned to see what appeared to be a driverless car barreling toward them and yelled, "What the fuck?" as he leapt into the air and onto the hood of the car. Bogey, seeing the look of terror on Skeeter's face, quickly determined that it was better for the car to hit the guy in the wheelchair unimpeded by him acting as a human shield and he also dove on top of the car, causing both of them to slide into the front seat on top of a half-naked woman. This tumultuous entry resulted in the vehicle making a sharp left turn, thereby avoiding most of the horrified screaming citizens and becoming lodged underneath the double-decker deluxe Porta Potty that had been rented for the event. It did not, however, prevent a crazed stampede by the audience toward the front from trampling the first couple of rows of assembled dignitaries.

The collapsed governor had diverted the attention of the participants, and it wasn't until Ingrid looked up to see a mass of humanity coming upon them like a tsunami and screeched, "Sweet Jesus, have mercy" that anyone realized the danger they were in. Ron, Montavious and Brooke were seated front and center in attached chairs that were unceremoniously dumped as a group in unison by the onslaught of humanity behind them. Red, recognizing the opportunity for escape presented by the chaos, grabbed as many abandoned gift bags as he could hold and beat it out the back way, leaving behind Ingrid to fend for herself. Bedlam prevailed. Actually, Ingrid had tripped over the flattened governor, whose outstretched profile was quite similar to that of a beached manatee, causing a domino effect, whereby Boone fell into familiar territory on top of Brooke, and Berdenna ended up spread eagle on her back leaving nothing to the imagination including her red and black Mistress of the Night panties. Jaap had made a run toward the Pop-Tart table only to become impaled on the top of the wheelchair of Mrs. Ephigenia Porzingis, chairwoman of the Society of Daughters of the Latvian Revolution. Flailing away on top of Mrs. Porzingis, he was finally able to extricate himself from the crumpled heap of humankind and seized on the political opportunity to beeline it to a TV camera.

"Senator, can you tell us what happened?"

"Yes, I was with the others in prayer when this terrorist attack was launched against all we hold sacred. It was only through the brave, fearless action of those two men in the back that we didn't have something on the order of another 9/11."

"Do you know who was behind this?"

"Not sure now, but I plan to hold hearings on this when I get back to Lansing. We will need to determine whether this was the act of a lone wolf who has been radicalized over the internet or whether we have a sleeper cell imbedded in Glenn."

"Where is the governor, and is he okay?"

"The governor was steadfast during all of this. He appeared to get some sort of security alert on his phone and instead of falling back as others did, he went forward. I anticipate he will be calling out the National Guard to help hunt down any co-conspirators."

"Senator, one last question: You appear quite bruised and battered. Did the terrorist reach you?"

"No, thank God, but realizing the extreme danger of the situation, I presented myself as a shield for the disabled who had been rendered helpless by the havoc created by the heathen attack."

"Thank you, senator. This is Poppy McBride reporting from Glenn for Channel 2 Action News."

Bogey and Skeeter had been knocked unconscious when the Subaru collided with the Porta Potty. The impact had the opposite effect on Matilda, who was just becoming cognizant of the fact that she was half-naked in a convertible with two guys on top of her looking at a sign that said, "Remove Waste Here." Instinctively she crawled out of the car and began to run, stopping only to rip a tablecloth off the buffet table to use as a wrap, causing eye witnesses to report seeing a Klan-like figure fleeing the scene. Meanwhile, Skeeter and Bogey were slowing reviving, surrounded by a scrum of reporters, microphones and cameras. Cable news networks were flashing their photos and identifying them as the mystery heroes of the day. Even the White House press office issued a statement citing them as two stalwarts who stood between terror and the American people. The president's political staff concurrently began to debate where they should be seated during the next State of the Union address.

Disheveled and discombobulated, the press swarmed them, and questions were flying everywhere. Skeeter did all the talking.

"Gentlemen, did you know this attack was coming?"

"Well, ma'am, in the Boy Scouts I learned always to be prepared."

"Did you get a good look at the perpetrator?"

"Yes, I did get a good look, if you know what I mean."

"Did you ever fear for your life?"

"Yes, the time I stole my second cousin's cooler of Bud Light."

"When did you realize you were in danger?"

"When the car hit me."

"Do you plan to participate in the search for the perpetrator?"

"Yes, when it appears on *America's Most Wanted.*"

"Any words of advice for your fellow Americans on how to stay safe?"

"Obey the speed limit."

Even before the networks were able to identify the two heroes, the Department of Homeland Security had received a call from a woman named Norma Jean at the Waffle House in Hahira, Georgia, identifying the two as Bogey Jackson and Skeeter Williams. Her quick action resulted in her being named Waffle House Employee of the Month and a guest appearance on the *Crimestoppers* TV show.

Meanwhile, Bogey in his Smith & Wesson hat caught the attention of the company's headquarters in Springfield, Massachusetts, and they immediately dispatched a PR flak to offer him a six-figure contract as national spokesman for their "Shoot First, Then Ask" advertising campaign. Skeeter, on the other hand, was approached by Critter Control to initiate a new promotional campaign called "Make America Great and Vermin Free." The two boys from Hahira had hit the big time.

TWENTY-SEVEN

J ack Hightower was a mangled mess buried under a pile of bodies, all whom were letting out collective groans. First to extricate himself from the pile had been Red Johansson, who was now nowhere to be seen. He had been followed by Jaap VanValkenberg who could be heard pontificating in the distance with a gaggle of reporters. Sean and Paddy were first to come to the rescue and were very indelicately pulling bodies apart in the heap. Berdenna came out feet first with her skirt pulled up to her chest, showing all her glory. Next a very disheveled Montavious yelling, "I will get those mother-fuckers," followed by the Reverend Ingrid, miter askew, and still sprinkling holy water and prophesizing, "God works in mysterious ways." Ron had hit himself on the head with his briefcase and was lying prone over the still-collapsed governor, giving the appearance he was trying to mate the manatee, while Boone and Brooke were intertwined in a motionless embrace. All-in-all, it was a cluster fuck!

"Grab the big-titted one by the feet so we can get the old one below," instructed Sean to Paddy as they pulled on Berdenna.

"Shit, she is heavy, but looking at her panties makes me think she must be a real sport. Maybe she will pay us back in kind when this is all over," responded Paddy with a mind that never left the gutter.

"Look at these two. If they weren't unconscious, I would tell them to go get a room. I think it is the CEO dude and that hot pistol he trots around with. Someone told me she was once a Dallas Cowboys cheerleader. She sure would inspire me to score a touchdown. Just push him to the side so he doesn't suffocate the poor babe."

Slowly the pile of people began to unravel with Paddy and Sean leading the effort. Getting to the bottom, they found Jack, who thought he had finally met his maker.

"God bless you, boys. I never thought I would get out from underneath. What the hell happened?"

"Well, sir, it was a missile-like attack carefully executed. Our boss, Senator VanValkenberg, believes it was a terrorist attack, probably Al Qaeda, intended to undercut our free enterprise system by impeding the flow of government money to private companies. A strike at the very heart of what we are all about. Why, just think there would be nowhere for the NFL or MLB to play without taxpayer support."

"You fellows really get it. You say you work for Senator VanValkenberg. What brings you to Glenn constituents outreach?"

"Sort of, the MEDC has agreed to fund a National Political Corruption Hall of Fame, and we have been hired under the Irish Americans Reparations Act to staff it. We are down here scouting out a location. Sure hope this incident doesn't derail our plans."

"Young men, I don't think you realize who you are talking to. I am the chairman of the MEDC, and I can assure you after the bravery you have exhibited today, the Hall of Fame will go forward and, in fact, I plan to recommend we increase our support for the project to make sure it's a success. By the way, you don't know Ms. Audrey Richenberg, who is also starting a business in this area?"

"Not really, but if we need to find her, just let us know."

Meanwhile, Red, carrying an armful of gift bags, had finally distanced himself far enough from the scene that he felt comfortable enough taking a rest. The two rednecks from Georgia were nowhere to be seen, and whatever had happened clearly had spared him from being viciously attacked by the two malcontents. His plan was to lay low here for a while and then double back after the Channel 2 Eye in the Sky helicopter had left the scene, figuring Bogey and Skeeter would have left for the free food at the community center.

Hunkered down in the bushes, he peeped out to see a vaguely familiar woman with mousy-brown hair wrapped in a tablecloth singing, "Off to See the Wizard," come strolling down the pathway. She looked like Dorothy on downers. Red knew he had seen her before, but where and when and what the hell was she doing here now?

"Hey, lady, over here," barked Red, startling the Judy Garland wannabe.

"Who called me? Are you the wizard?" replied Matilda in a state of delirium brought on by an overdose of marijuana-infused Girl Scout S'mores and severe blows to her head.

Red, realizing she was totally toasted, responded, "It is me — over here. I am performing a rear-guard action to protect us from another attack from this direction. Come join me."

With that, the tablecloth-cloaked woman plopped down next to Red and pulled out a handful of Girl Scout S'mores from her pants pocket.

"Want one? They are a prescription from the Glenn Apothecary but glad to share. They really cure what ails ya'. Sort of makes you one with the cosmos."

Finally, Red realized who she was. She was the do-gooder Executive Director of the Coalition of Concerned Citizens for Transparent and Ethical Government, an organization that was the bane of every group trying to wallow in the government trough. She was simply a pain in the ass to all trying to perfect the public-private partnership model on behalf of voracious capitalism system. Her apparent fugue state made Red realize he may have come upon an opportunity.

"Are you Matilda Hoffenmeister, Executive Director of the Coalition of Concerned Citizens for Transparent and Ethical Government? I have been a great fan of you and your organization for years. What brings you to Glenn today?"

"Let me tell you a little secret. I was here to see my boyfriend the governor for a little whoop-de-do. We keep quiet about our relationship for political reasons — optics and all. But that ol' blubber ball is really a pile driving man. Together we transcend political stereotypes."

"Well, isn't that interesting. You have given me an idea. Maybe you and your boyfriend may want to discreetly join my wife and me in a water-recovery recycling program that we are about to begin here in Glenn under the auspices of the Wave of the Future Church, where my wife is the minister. Our plan is to take the essence of life — water — and make it available to the masses as an ecumenical redistribution of our natural resources. The fact that you and Handkerchief have become silent partners will be our little secret."

"What would you need us to do? The governor is a man of high ethical standards, and my involvement would be predicated on what is best for the consumers and the environment. I will say the redistribution of anything is a cause I have wholeheartedly supported ever since leaving the Bernie Sanders campaign."

"Beautiful. What we need the two of you to do is very simple. You and your organization will need to defend us from attacks by those who want to continue the concentration of our natural resources in the hands of a few. As far as big boy is concerned, he needs to make sure that the Department of Environmental Quality stays out of our way."

"Well, what is it you are actually going to do?"

"Sell bottled water we pump from Lake Michigan."

"Holy shit!"

"You'll love it. Have another S'more, ditch that tablecloth and wrap yourself in these oak vines. We need to get out of here."

TWENTY-EIGHT

Berdenna's panties were in a wad literally and figuratively. She had planned to feature her recently purchased red and black Mistress of the Night thong as an accoutrement at the opening of her new business, a fashion statement she would market through an adjoining gift shop. However, after being dragged from the pile feet first by Sean and Paddy, her thong was in shreds. Hopefully, the Victoria Secret store next to the Cheetah Club in Grand Rapids would have another size XXL.

Not only was she disconsolate over what was to be part of her opening-day garb, but she was quickly realizing what an opportunity was being loss by not capitalizing on all this national attention in Glenn. Still slightly dazed and abandoned by her husband, who was ensconced in front of the TV cameras, she determined decisive action was in order.

"Mr. Hightower, I don't know if you remember me, but I accompanied Ms. Audrey Richenberg in Lansing to attend the Michigan Economic Development Commission which you chaired and at which an incentive package was approved for DGMG."

"Well, of course I remember. That meeting is etched in my memory. I didn't realize you were Senator Van Valkenberg's wife. He is a great American!" responded Chairman Hightower still staggering from what all knew was a terrorist attack.

"Where is Ms. Richenberg?" he inquired with his libido firmly in charge.

"I have just spoken with her, and she is adamant that we will not be cowered by this attack on what we all stand for. She is willing to immediately commence business as a message to the terrorist that free enterprise will not be intimidated, but will need you to expedite the incentive package in order to proceed. Why Mr. Hightower, God and country call us into action."

"Ms. VanValkenberg, I am duty bound to honor your request and am ordering by executive tweet the MEDC to immediately transfer $450,000 from the Female Venture Capital Fund to DGMG and to issue you a restaurant license effective today. This license will also exempt you from any of those burdensome health and safety regulations. I assume Ms. Richenberg will be there when you open?"

"Mr. Hightower, thank you for your patriotic fervor. The message that Glenn is open for business will be heard around the world. Your ability to cut red tape should make us able to open tomorrow and, yes, Ms. Richenberg will be there. Can you join us?"

"Once again, duty dictates that I attend. Just tell me what time and I will be there. Anything else you need?"

"No, I am fairly equipped other than a couple of coffee pots."

"Huh?" was the only response from a confused but excited Jack Hightower.

While Jaap continued to pontificate with the press, Sean and Paddy roused the semi-comatose governor and, unbeknownst to him, they commandeered his iPhone and declared a state of emergency by a tweet to the commander of the National Guard with a cc to Channel 2 Action News. They then forwarded the emergency tweet to the chairman and staff of the Michigan Economic Development Commission and once again, using the governor's phone, ordered them to "without undue delay immediately implement all pending incentive applications in the Glenn area and continue to do so until Homeland Security determines that the attack on our institutions has been thwarted."

Talk about setting the stage to pluck the government goose! They were now positioned to cash in for the National Political Corruption Hall of Fame and also whatever mindless flow of dough that would come out of the Federal Emergency Management Agency to address this lakeshore disaster. This could be the mother lode of government cash, but they would need to act quickly.

The first thing was to have an intern from Senator VanValkenberg's office dispatched to the commission office with a letter written by the intern and "signed" by the senator demanding immediate release of all "funding and inducements directed at the creation of a National Political Corruption Hall of Fame." This in turn provided for a cash injection into the nascent checking account of the Hall of Fame, and they also ordered the immediate transfer the old car barn building across from the DGMG project to the ownership of the soon-to-be opened hall.

Now to fill it, Paddy immediately called his cousin Mick back in Chicago and offered him two cases of Old Milwaukee beer if he would go to his parents' house and gather his Whitey Bulger Fan Club material and bring it to Glenn. Meanwhile, Sean began to design the Jack Abramoff bar sleaze scene, where someday it would interactively enable those touring the hall to hand cash to politicians while buying them drinks. For the time being, the scene would be static with a life-size cutout of Abramoff holding his Blackberry and a bag of cash next to an inebriated inflatable caricature of a rotund, cigar-smoking senator. Completing the exhibit was to be a section dedicated to Wilbur Mills and Fanne Foxe, aka the Argentine firecracker, later to be known as the Tidal Basin Bombshell after their drunken escapade in D.C. — years ago. Listed as the #3 sex scandal in political history by Bloomberg News, the exhibit would consist of a picture of Congressman Wilbur Mills chairing the Ways and Means

Committee, juxtaposed with Fanne's *Playboy* spread and background music from the Broadway hit *Evita*. All that was needed were a few American flags out front, a picture of the governor and Senator VanValkenberg with campaign bunting in the window and the official seal of the Coalition for Lobbying and Ethics in Government. In less than 24 hours, the Hall of Fame was ready to open, and it looked like it might coincide with Berdenna's new business across the street.

Berdenna was moving with alacrity. The two Mr. Coffee machines she had lifted from the Garden of Peace Rest Home while visiting Audrey would do just fine. Styrofoam cups with the company slogan" Dream Big" were easily pilfered from the Mattress Mart store. It was the signage that was critical and would take some doing. She decided to swing by Home Depot and pick up plywood, poles, spray paint and stencils for lettering. Realizing she would need some extra manpower, she then swung by the handyman staffing company to see if she might hire a couple of day laborers who could be paid for under her Lansing grant. As luck would have it, two methed-out workers remained and both went only by their last names. First was Kowalski, who claimed he had spent the last year trying to get enough bus money to visit his dying mother in Chicago and the other was Umbango, a Congolese refugee seeking asylum in America from his strife-torn homeland, of which he had no idea as to why it was strife-torn or even where the Congo was.

Pole digging and cobbling the signs together was the first order of business. Meanwhile, Berdenna stenciled on the lettering and spray painted them. Dusk was settling in and in order to keep Kowalski and Umbango focused on the task at hand, she went out and bought a case of Boones Farm Orange Pineapple wine, which seemed to do the trick. The signs were completed just before the two-day laborers passed out for the night. The highway version identified the Glenn exit as the home of "Chesty Treasures Stimulating Beanery — Better than an Oriental Massage."

The storefront sign read a little different, "Chesty Treasures Stimulating Beanery — Where a Big Gulp Comes with an Eyeful Every Time" and finally the red, white and blue banner over the entrance promised "Two Drive-Thru's for the Price of One."

Now that the signs were in place, Berdenna felt comfortable doing one last promotional tweet: "Opening tomorrow. Chesty Treasures Stimulating Beanery — Where You Always Get Two at a Time." This tweet received by Mr. Jack Hightower made him very excited realizing Ms. Audrey Richenberg, CEO of DGMG would be there.

Audrey would be there. and Berdenna decided to once again take advantage of her dissociative identity disorder, which caused her to think she was Marilyn Monroe. What better eye-catcher than a re-enactment of the blowing skirt scene over the grate prior to the movie *The Seven Year Itch*. It was iconic. Sure, Audrey was not exactly in her prime, but she would be more effective than those wildly gyrating inflatables you see everywhere, and all she needed was a large fan, a low-cut dress and an apple crate to stand on. Maybe throw in a parasol for added effect.

"Audrey — I'm sorry, I mean Marilyn — this is Berdenna. You are needed tomorrow to do a promo for your new movie, *The Seven Year Itch*. The director wants you to wear a white, low-cut dress than will billow in the wind. Can you make it?"

"Of course, darling. Will Joe or any of my other husbands be there?"

"Sure, I think I can arrange for Joe to be there if that would make you more comfortable. How about I pick you up at 6:45 a.m.?"

"I will be ready."

The Joe DiMaggio piece necessitated another call and some not-so-subtle political pressure.

"Hi, is this the Western Michigan University Theatre Department? This is Berdenna VanValkenberg, wife of Senator Jaap VanValkenberg who sits on the Higher Education Appropriations Committee. Could I borrow that Joe DiMaggio cutout prop you used last year in the play *Boys of Summer?* (Quiet) Thanks, I will be right over to pick it up."

Berdenna, as the barista, knew the main attraction would be a cup of java delivered at the drive-through window in a memorable fashion. Her business courses at Calvin had taught her how important asset management was, and she intended to utilize them to the fullest. Invoking her Dutch heritage, she purchased a Dutch-maid outfit with the shortest of skirts, red clogs and topped off with a classic bonnet with triangular flaps with nothing between the hat and the skirt. She was about to open the first state-funded topless drive-through coffee shop.

Chairman Hightower was tingling with excitement over the thought of seeing Ms. Audrey Richenberg again. The ol' gray fox had been lusting after her since that first meeting in Lansing, and the opening this morning he was confident would result in a roll in the hay. Better be prepared. He gulped down a double-dose of Viagra with his prune juice expecting those two blue pills to kick in just about the time he arrived in Glenn. His anticipation was such that he couldn't help but continually belt out on the drive down, "The fire engine is coming, the pump is primed and the siren is on!"

TWENTY-NINE

R ed saw an opportunity in all the confusion. Whatever the hell had happened back there sure was creating chaos, and in the midst of that no one would notice an innocuous septic system truck making a stop in the middle of an abandoned golf course. Probably just cleaning up the mess of some derelict super-fund site.

Action was in order. He and Matilda would need to work their way back to where the groundbreaking had been underway, but first he would have to find some kind of top for Matilda to replace the oak leaves serving as a cover. Luckily, he spotted a faded "Drill, Baby, Drill — Sarah Palin for Vice President" T-shirt hanging on a backyard clothesline. Not a perfect fit, but close enough for her to wear. Now they were good to go.

First stop was the Glenn Apothecary where Red could trade in a series of 50% off coupons acquired in the purloined gift bags. Keeping Matilda stoked up on Girl Scout S'mores from the store was a critical component of his plan.

"Rosa, what happened back at the groundbreaking site? I found Matilda here in a state of stupor but was able to extricate her to a place of safety."

"Without question, a terrorist attack," responded Rosa. "The governor has declared a state of emergency. The Coast Guard is on 24-hour patrol, and Anderson Cooper of CNN is expected to arrive any minute. Thank God you were able to rescue Matilda. She was in earlier today, and it is critical her meds don't run out."

"That is why I am here. I have five 50% off coupons for Girl Scout S'mores and thought I would get some of those dozen economy packs. I imagine 60 hits should last her a couple of days."

"Agree, that should last her a while. Let me go to the back room and get what you need. Back in a minute."

Just then, on a flat screen TV hung over the tranquilizer display, Bret Baier of Fox News announced that they were switching back to their D.C. studio for an exclusive interview with a twosome who had been dubbed the Hahira Heroes. Sure enough, there in all their glory stood Bogey Jackson and Skeeter Williams with a backdrop of the Pentagon behind them.

"Gentlemen, the nation is indebted to you for your courageous action in preventing another terrorist attack. This time in the very heartland."

Causing a puzzled Skeeter to ask, "Like, they owe us money?"

"Well, not exactly. Understand you have been asked to brief the Military Preparedness Team of the Joint Chiefs on tactical methods. Exactly what advice will you be giving them?"

"Shoot, then aim. Works every time. You can clear out an entire trailer park in minutes," advised Bogey.

"Thank you, gentlemen. We are out of time. Back after this message from Rolaids."

Eureka! With Bogey and Skeeter hundreds of miles away, the coast was clear to return to the site. He had enough "medicine" to keep Matilda in a perpetual haze, and now he could implement his plan with a couple of phone calls.

"Good morning, Hoekstra Septic and Well Drilling. May I help you?"

"Hi, this is Red Johansson. Is Virg in?"

"Just a minute and I will check."

"Hi Red, Virg here. Are you okay? I heard about that terrorist attack in Glenn and immediately thought of you. What happened?"

"It was terrible. Might have been Al Qaeda, ISIS or the Muslim Brotherhood. We just don't know yet. What we do know is that the world is watching, and we must show them that we will not be intimidated. The governor has asked that we ramp up our activities in a show of defiance."

"Well, what can I do to help?"

"Remember that side contract I procured for you with the Department of Environmental Quality to assist the new Wave of the Future Church? The one where you would install pumps and piping from the church grounds to Lake Michigan in order to facilitate the state water redistribution program? Well, it seems to me the patriotic thing to do would be for you to come by tomorrow and install the system. Plus, by the way, you will be able to double-bill the state under the Emergency Action Emolument Order."

"You got my attention with that double-billing provision. I have always said freedom isn't free, and patriotism has a price. See you in the morning."

Matilda in tow, clutching her five economy-size boxes of Girl Scout S'mores, Red headed back to where the carnage had taken place. The governor, surrounded by a phalanx of aides, continued in a stupefied state seated on a lawn chair, unsure where he was or what had happened. Boone, Brooke, Montavious and Ron had all piled into the back of the limo after having been instructed by corporate security to find a safe haven. Montavious was calling an ol' buddy who had been a protégé of Stokely Carmichael and was now trying to reconstitute the Black Panther Party from his basement in Quincy, Illinois, with funds from an Urban Development Action Grant (UDAG). Montavious suggested that if he organized an affiliate in Glenn, they might be able to bill Homeland Security for the protection of the ERR LLC pipe.

Meanwhile, Brooke was making it quite clear to Boone that if they were not airborne in the company jet post haste, their days of pretend, part-time connubial bliss would be over. Also, there was no question that a stop at Neiman Marcus upon arrival back in Dallas was on the agenda to replace her tattered outfit.

Ron was on the phone with his mother.

Back at the ceremony site, Ingrid could be seen kneeling by the ERR LLC pipe. The attack and resultant blow to the head had placed her in a permanent state of religious chimera. Chanting in tongues and waving her arms toward the sky, she was oblivious to her surroundings. Red approached cautiously and after explaining that he was a disciple, he was able to coax her back to the old abandoned golf course clubhouse by telling her she was needed back at the church to tend to her flock.

Red, surveying the scene, doubted anyone would notice or care why Hoekstra Septic was laying new pipe at the scene of a day-old terrorist attack. Just to be safe, however, one way to insure no snooping bureaucrats got in the way would be to have the governor present at the event.

"Matilda, is there any way you think you could get the governor here tomorrow to attend our religious patriotic pipe laying?"

Matilda, who by this time was already through her first box of S'mores, appeared close to an OD crash. The governor still surrounded by a gaggle of people had no idea she was just across the field.

"I think so," she slurred. "Watch this."

She pulled out her iPhone with the Snapchat app, found the topless selfie she had previously sent to the governor and typed in, "This and more, big boy, if you come back in the morning" and pressed resend.

Moments later shrieks could be heard from around the governor and screams for medical help. Turns out the governor for some reason had pulled out his cell phone, checked the screen, rose from his chair in a profuse sweat and executed the second face plant of the day, this time into a portal defibrillator positioned by the medics.

Quickly gurneyed to an arriving ambulance, he was heard making the MacArthur-like statement, "I will return."

THIRTY

Business was brisk at the Glenn Apothecary. Despite, or maybe because of the turmoil created by the terrorist attack the day before, long lines stood outside waiting for them to open. Why, in the first 15 minutes, Dr. Violin performed almost a dozen physicals, and most of these new customers came in with 50% off coupons in hand. The opening of two new businesses along with the presence of TV trucks and a gaggle of network anchors and reporters made tiny Glenn a happening place.

The town's notoriety was greatly enhanced by the fact that two guys known as the Hahira Heroes had performed what only could be called gallant patriotic unselfish acts in Glenn and now were nationally recognized as hosts of *America's Most Wanted* TV show, sponsored jointly by Smith & Wesson and Critter Control. The two heroes, often referred to as America's best, were the subject of numerous articles and TV specials extolling them as role models for the nation's youth and as Make America Great Again kind of men. They quickly capitalized on their newfound fame and fortune by purchasing 10 struggling Waffle Houses in Southeast Georgia and placing an unknown business woman named Norma Jean Boatmen in charge as CEO. They also simultaneously created a philanthropic foundation, which, for some unknown reason, would hand out free Costco membership cards to the hungry and homeless. They were national sensations.

The uptick in business at the apothecary was nothing compared with what was going on only a block away. A massive line of cars and trucks had formed waiting to visit the new drive-through coffee shop. The line snaked its way for over a mile back to the interstate. It seemed like every 18-wheeler in Southwest Michigan was on its way and, in fact, they were. The turnout was being driven by the anonymous posting on social media of a picture of a big-titted Dutch woman serving coffee with the tagline 'Stop by Glenn and See More.' The photo had gone from Facebook to Twitter and then finally to the website lonelytruckers.com, where it had so many hits and likes that the site collapsed. Compounding the congestion were the number of gawking passersby stopping to look at the 90-year-old gyrating woman standing on an apple crate with a fan-induced billowing skirt, brandishing a parasol and bellowing out show tunes. Further complicating the matter was a rumor that for some unknown reason the governor and the chairman of the Michigan Economic Development Commission were making a return visit to Glenn.

While all the commotion was under way downtown, two large Hoekstra Septic and Well Drilling trucks lumbered through, headed toward the old abandoned golf course/church grounds. The site had overnight been designated a national priority one security zone and was being guarded by two Andy Frain Rent-a-Cops on loan from bleacher duty at Wrigley Field.

"Halt! Who goes there?" barked the rent-a-cop as Virg pulled up in the lead truck while the Andy Frain Rent-a-Cop twirled his baton in a menacing fashion.

"Virg Hoekstra. Me and my guys in the back are under emergency orders from the government to immediately commence drilling as a result of the recent terrorist attack."

"What are their names and do you have any documentation proving this order?" demanded the rent-a-cop.

"Sure, their names are Mohammed and Yusef, and here are my official government papers." With that, he pulled out a Certificate of Recognition emblazoned with the state seal he had received from Senator Jaap VanValkenberg four years before, which read:

"Certificate of Recognition to Hoekstra Septic and Well Drilling for cleaning up the crap no one else will touch."

The rent-a-cop was duly impressed, and his reaction confirmed when a woman in a Sarah Palin Drill, Baby, Drill T-shirt sauntered up and announced that the governor was on his way to personally oversee the drilling and that Virg, Mohammed and Yusef were to be admitted immediately. Now convinced, the two Andy Frain guards waved them through, mounted their Vespas and escorted them to the well site where Red was waiting.

"Virg — over here. Sure is good to see you."

"Well, it was my patriotic duty to be here as quick as possible, and you got my attention when you said I could double bill for the project."

"Here's the deal," directed Red. "I want you to install a big damn pipe with a strong pump next to that oil leaking contraption going to Lake Michigan and then another pipe from here to the abandoned golf clubhouse, which is now the Wave of the Future Church. Cost is of no object since all bills will go to the Department of Environmental Quality, plus the governor is on the way to visit with ol' pump queen here (pointing at Matilda idly popping Girl Scout Happy S'mores), and you can be assured he will approve every cost."

"What if he doesn't?"

"Don't worry, he will. Drilling will be on his mind, but not the kind you are doing."

"Well, hell, if that is the case, I may need to staff up. I will bring on my two teenage nephews as 'virtual technical advisors' and my grandmother in the same vein as part of Senior Citizen Outreach."

"Sounds good to me," responded Red. "Whatever it takes to get this job done quickly and before anyone notices what is going on here. Let it rip."

The Andy Frain security team concluded that an extra layer or two of security might be in order and immediately parked their Vespas sideways at the entrance as a barrier to another attack. They also doubled down by rolling out two more rows of crime scene tape as a deterrent.

Virg, comfortable that the scene was secure, contacted his grandmother and two nephews to alert them that they were now employed on the project, but their presence was not necessary since they would be billed as virtual employees. None of them had any idea of what he was talking about but liked the idea of no-show government work.

It was about a quarter of a mile to Lake Michigan, but without any nitpicking regulators to impede progress, the undertaking would be a piece of cake. Sure, he might have to bore through a few aquifers that could collapse later resulting in sinkholes and cliff erosion, but that would take months if not years, and he would be long gone. Just to be safe, he could also get Senator VanValkenberg to introduce post-facto legislation indemnifying Hoekstra Company from any liability. What was a little environmental damage when you are talking jobs!

Virg and his two assistants, Mohammed and Yusef, immediately got to work with Grandma and the two nephews clocking in from home. Yusef mounted the borrowed RT120 ditch witch trencher which he had learned to operate in the Syrian Army and was able to burrow a path to the beach in short order. Some damage was done to a field of endangered Michigan monkey-flowers and significant damage to a major aquifer, but luckily it was unnoticeable to the untrained eye. The pipe was quickly laid and covered unobtrusively, except for the portion of pipe sticking up in the water in Lake Michigan about 10 yards offshore. Red realized this random pipe might become a point of curiosity, so he had the Hoekstra team surround it with floating buoys and place a sign about which read in English and Spanish:

National Oceanic and Atmospheric Administration Lake Level Test Site. Protected under U.S. Code Section 1022 and 1025. Trespassers subject to fines and life in prison. Have a happy day at the beach.

Sitio de prueba del nivel del lago de la Administracion Nacional Oceanic y Atmosferica. Protegido bajo U.S. codigo seccion 1022 y 1025. Intrusos sujeto a multas y cadena perpetua. Que tengas un feliz dia en la playa.

Laying the pipe to the Wave of the Future Church was a little bit trickier. No question it would require the destruction of the habitat of the threatened northern long-eared bat on the way. For this, Virg had some pangs of guilt, but then he rationalized, 'What the hell, a few less bats, a few more mosquitos, but as long as Off was still readily available in local drugstores no harm done.'

As Virg and the boys neared the clubhouse/church, Ingrid could be seen standing on top of the rusted golf club drop-off stand bedecked in her tattered pastoral robe, miter askew, but adorned with a new pectoral cross she had picked up at a Greek Orthodox Church yard sale. Her delusional state as a High Priest was now permanently imbued in her psyche since the trauma of the terrorist attack. A condition that was fine with Red since it made the implementation of his scheme that much easier.

Tugging a stupefied Matilda behind him, Red approached the crusading Ingrid.

"Ingrid, what a glorious day to open our new church. It has been a long time coming, but our faith in the Lord has been fulfilled."

"Yes, Red, and from this day on, I am ready to leave the material world behind and dedicate myself and this endeavor to the spiritual realm."

"I know you are, dear, and as I began to reflect on the Wave of the Future Church, its name and mission reminded me of **Psalm 8:8-11** which speaks to waves, water and their role in God's kingdom and how we can share them with all of his creatures."

"Forgive me, Red, but I am not familiar with **Psalm 8:8-11**. Pray tell, what is it?"

"Red then unwrapped a 10-foot square sign with gold letters: *The birds of the heaven and the fish of the sea, whatever passes along the paths of the seas. This far you may come and no farther; here is where your proud waves halt. —* **Psalm 8:8-11**. *"*

"Oh, Red, that is beautiful. What a lovely sign for out on the road beckoning all to join us. What are the two smaller signs?"

He then pulled out two smaller signs with red lettering and adorned with crosses that could be hung on hooks under the Psalm.

The first one read: *Come and Get Your Piece of the Wave Only $5!* The second one to be hung beneath it read: *Refills Half Price!*

Red had pulled off the unimaginable. Every economic developer's dream. He had used government incentives to create a tax-free entity that would use the common resource of Lake Michigan at no cost to him to bottle and sell water.

Doesn't get any sweeter than that.

THIRTY-ONE

Governor Baumgarten awoke in his official residence back in Lansing in a heavy sweat. His infatuation with Matilda compelled him to check his Snapchat account almost hourly to assure himself that her selfie was still there. In the middle of the night, realizing lust conquers all, he determined it was time to emulate his hero and fellow governor of South Carolina. That morning at practically dawn, gulping down two Cinnabons for fortification and sustenance, he ordered his state trooper driver to put on the lights and siren and head back to Glenn.

Meanwhile, Jack Hightower was also ripping down the highway to Glenn blasting on his cassette player the 60s hit song "Wild Thing" by the Troggs, getting him more and more excited as he belted out "Wild thing, you make everything groovy." He was getting a little concerned that the two Viagra pills he had popped had not quite kicked in yet, and God forbid he would arrive and not be ready for action. What the hell, he popped another one.

Just about this time Jack heard a siren and saw flashing lights in his rear-view mirror. It was a black Chevy SUV that had the unmistakable markings of the governor's car. Why in the world would the governor be headed back to Glenn, he had no idea. Maybe a briefing on the terrorist incident. Regardless, this presented an opportunity. As the Chevy passed him on the left, he could see the governor pouring sweat, mopping his brow and looking down on his iPhone. Jack honked causing the clearly agitated governor to look up, but upon seeing his economic development chairman, he gave a thumbs up, which Jack interpreted as the okay to change lanes and ease into his slipstream for a high speed run to Glenn. Two dogs in heat on a mission.

Governor Baumgarten knew in his heart it was time to implement what he had dubbed the "Sanford Plan," after his gubernatorial buddy. The two had met at a Christian Values Family Conference, where the then Governor of South Carolina told Earl that he was seeking a higher calling, which he eventually found in the form of an Argentine bombshell. An affair ensued, subsidized by the taxpayers of South Carolina, culminating in a tearful but exalted exit from office. Earl knew with Matilda on the horizon, and the scrutiny he was under in Lansing the moment was here. Turns out the state attorney general, Elliott Dodge — heir to the auto fortune, fellow Republican and like all attorney generals, an aspiring governor — was threatening to expose the governor's repeated use of his state credit card at the Hotsy Totsy Club in Lansing. The governor had defended the use of the card as normal "constituent out-reach," but when the surcharge appeared for a "private lap dance," it became more difficult to defend.

The governor had developed his departure plan with the assistance of Clive Bansley, a retired Navy admiral who operated a dilapidated WWII amphibious vehicle called a duck boat for tourists. Governor Baumgarten had helped Clive get his vessel included in the Maritime Security Program, funded by the U.S. Department of Transportation, intended to have ships available in time of war. Having a retired admiral was great for optics and he clearly qualified under the requirement it be operated by U.S. citizens, and the war preparation clause was fulfilled by the need described on the application as "ready should a naval attack from Canada occur." The $1.1 million subsidy awarded the admiral kept him comfortable in retirement, and he was diligent in keeping the vessel sea-worthy by hosting Sunday afternoon cruises with his wife's quilting club.

"Clive, this is Governor Baumgarten. I am on the way to Glenn and wondered whether your ship might be available for a national security undertaking to Wisconsin?"

"Of course, sir. After reading about the terrorist attack, I thought I might be called into duty so I had both tanks topped off and the galley loaded with provisions of Pop-Tarts, Cheez-Its, and Chips Ahoy Cookies."

"How long would it take to get to Racine?"

"Well, we average about 15 knots per hour, so assuming no headwinds or heavy seas a short 5 hours."

"Short 5 hours?"

"As opposed to long."

"Oh, I see. Well, this has to be kept top secret, but when I text you "time to waddle," I want you to come ashore on the beach near the old golf course and be prepared to take two of us on a clandestine mission to Racine. Got it?"

"Aye, aye, governor."

Jack Hightower was making record time to Glenn in the slipstream of the governor's SUV, which was good since the triple dose of Viagra was kicking in and he was tiring of "Wild Thing." He had spent many sleepless nights tossing, turning and mulling over his unrequited desire for Audrey. He knew this was true love and with the proper proposal could entice her to elope with him so they could spend their golden years together. It finally dawned on him to call Merwyn Gladstone, his former deputy director at the commission. Merwyn had left a few years ago for Florida, where he had bought into a company that specialized in selling cemetery plots to WWI veterans. Merwyn had underestimated the law of supply and demand as the number of WWI veterans became exhausted and soon found himself unemployed, but through a friend at the cremation society secured a position as Director of Entertainment and Community Engagement at the Villages Retirement Complex.

"Merwyn, Jack Hightower here. How is it going down there?"

"Couldn't be better. I just negotiated and secured a tie-in with Preparation H that will give all of our residents 50% off when they buy a two pack."

"Where did you learn to become such a deal maker?"

"Cliff Notes of Trump's book *Art of the Deal*. Learned all about 'factual hyperbole' — used to be called lying, now just part of good negotiations. Works like a charm."

"Well, have I got a deal for you. How would you like to have an elderly starlet that does one mean Marilyn Monroe imitation? We are talking Branson level entertainment. She could be the star of your Ageless Beauties Revue."

"Sounds interesting. Where is she now and how much dough are we talking about?"

"Well, she is the main attraction at a posh resort on the lakeshore, but I imagine you could lure her away to sunny Florida with some free housing and meals. Now I would need to accompany her so maybe one of those condos overlooking the golf course would be nice and suitable for the two of us. What do you say? Straight barter deal. We get room, food and booze. You get a sexy ol' babe that will knock the socks off every Don Juan in the complex."

"You got a deal. If she's as hot as you say, maybe I can get a commission on the side from the local Cialis representative. She will work five days a week at the late-night happy hour, which is from 5 to 6 p.m. Tipping is permitted, so she is welcome to bring her own pole, whips, boots or whatever will arouse the crowd. Just let me know in advance so I can install some extra defibrillators."

"I will be back to you," replied an excited Jack Hightower.

Sean and Paddy were dispirited. Across the street at the coffee shop, long lines of trucks waited to be served and yet their National Political Corruption Hall of Fame was a ghost town. No spillover whatsoever. Sure, the ol' babe out front with the flapping skirt was eye-catching, but something else other than hot java was going on over there.

"Sean, we need to find out what the hell they are up to. That is either the damnedest coffee made or they got more than meets the eye."

"Well, I just can't walk up. Plus, that line stretches back for an hour, and if I try to butt in, one of those big truck drivers will beat the shit out of me."

"Here's an idea. Grab a six pack of that cheap rot-gut beer from the storage room refrigerator, saunter over to the cab of one of those trucks in line and offer the beer for a ride through the coffee line. Hell, there is not a trucker alive that wouldn't give you a lift for a six pack."

Sean liked the plan, so he grabbed a six pack of Hamm's Light and dashed across to the third truck in line, which had inscribed on the cab door "Mongoose in Residence. Beware."

Rapping on the door, he was met with a courteous, "What the fuck do you want?"

"Well, sir, my name is Sean O'Malley and I run the establishment across the street. We really need some coffee and I thought in exchange for this beer you might let me ride with you and order some coffee at the drive-through."

"Is it cold?"

"Sure is."

"Get your ass in here."

Once inside, Sean got a better look at his driver. Mongoose must have weighed 350 pounds. He had scraggly, long, greasy brown hair, a sleeveless T-shirt and on his biceps was the tattoo of a voluptuous woman and underneath her high heels it read, "Mongoose a pile driving man."

"Thank you, Mongoose. Appreciate the ride."

"Shut up and give me a beer."

"Sure, here you go. Just curious — what is so special about this coffee shop that has all you truckers lined up?"

"Tits."

"Huh, what do you mean tits?"

"Word is out on lonelytruckers.com that for the price of a cup of coffee you get to see the biggest set of knockers you could imagine."

Just then, Mongoose and Sean pulled up to the drive-through window to catch a sight that would have any straight male throbbing. There stood a topless Berdenna in her faux Dutch maid dress and cap and her size 44DD breasts in full splendor. On the right one, it was written in red magic marker, "50¢ extra — pull here for milk," and on the left one, "50¢ extra pull here for sugar."

"How may I help you, gentlemen?" she purred at Mongoose and Sean. "Black coffee is $3.95 a cup. Milk and sugar is extra, but see what you get for just 50¢?"

The sight of Berdenna resulted in Sean entering into a state of hyperventilation before he finally screamed out, "I will take two of everything," and with that dove across Mongoose's lap out the window grasping at the milk and sugar levers.

"No touching the merchandise until paid in full," chastised Berdenna, while swatting Sean's sweaty hands away.

The sudden rebuke from Berdenna caused Sean to jerk his head back into the cab with his face planted firmly in Mongoose's crotch. Mongoose thinking his manhood was under attack proceeded to repeatedly rap Sean's head with the empty Hamm's Light beer can, until he was unconscious.

Finally, Berdenna addressed Mongoose. "What will you have, big boy? By the way, if you order a double of everything, it comes with a picture of me as you see me now suitable for mounting on your dashboard."

"Shit, give me a triple!"

THIRTY-TWO

Boone, Brooke, Montavious and Ron clamored on to the Falcon 900 jet looking for escape and a safe haven from further terrorist attacks. Fleeing was the only option. Montavious had been unable to secure additional protection from his Black Panther comrade in Quincy. Brooke, always thinking ahead, had Googled Neiman Marcus in Dallas to make sure they would still be open when they arrived and then text messaged her personal shopper, Ashley Cupcake, to see if she might meet her at the private jet terminal. Boone realized the gravity of the situation and the attention it would bring to other ERR LLC tax fracking operations and emailed his personal company-provided criminal defense attorney, Sumnter Pendegrass, alerting him that the events could result in more unpleasant questions from the IRS. Ron called his mother to see if she might pick him up.

The company pilots had drilled for this type of event and were quite excited to actually be able to implement an escape plan. In preparation, they had reportedly watched the movie Argo about the escape of an American business-men from Iran and now felt as if their time had come. Terrorist attack, key corporate officers in danger, expedited departure — it didn't get any better than this!

"Team, in time of war you never know when it will be your last meal, so please pass the shrimp platter," advised Boone, trying to sound very CEO-ish. "Also, Ron open that bottle of Château Lafite, we must maintain a normal operating procedure. The stockholders would expect no less."

"Yes, sir."

"This tragedy provides us the impetus to reflect upon the company's goals, mission and objectives. A time of crisis can be an opportunity."

"So true," murmured Ron.

"I agree," chirped Brooke. "I just hope Ashley is there to meet me and that Neiman's is still open."

"What the fuck are you talking about?" barked Montavious.

What Boone's inner circle did not know was that Boone and ERR LLC was the focus of a Justice Department strike force looking into tax fraud, securities manipulation, corporate malfeasance and embezzlement. It was a case that made WorldCom and Bernie Ebbers look minor league. As a result, Boone had the company retain attorney Pendegrass who was the brother-in-law of the former Texas governor, now vice president, Horratio Thigpen. Sumnter Pendegrass proudly went by the moniker "back room," which was attributed to his ability to cut a deal no matter how nefarious the client. An ability that could be tested defending one Boone Cartwright.

Boone was looking at 10 to 20 years in the big house for corporate conduct so egregious that the former chairman of Tyco called it "aspirational white-collar crime." Sumnter had warned Boone against any other tax fracking initiatives, which, as he put it, "would further strain credulity" in the eyes of the IRS and the Justice Department. Now with Glenn and its attendant notoriety, Boone felt the strong arm of the law closing in on him.

Boone addressed his colleagues on the plane over a glass of Chateau Lafite. "The events of the past few hours have created an epiphany within me that I must share with you. I believe I have been called to a higher purpose in life."

Unbeknownst to the group, Boone had with Sumnter's counsel devised an exit strategy from ERR LLC, assuming a plea bargain with justice would be required. He also wanted to make sure he could do so with his ego and wallet intact.

Six months prior, through sleight-of-hand accounting, he had siphoned off a few million dollars of company assets to form a tax-free, ostensibly philanthropic entity called the "Faith in Our Future Fund." The fund was to be overseen by an independent board composed of Boone, his professional dog walker and his cleaning lady. Its purpose was to serve as "a resource for executive career development and other lawful purposes." In other words, it was a corporate slush fund he could spend on about anything he wanted, including keeping the silence of the three company officials accompanying him on the plane.

Sumnter had counseled Boone that one way to avoid serving 10 to 20 years in the slammer would be to cut a deal whereby he would establish an institute or the like dedicated to a lofty public policy goal where he might also employ Vice President Thigpen's ne'er-do-well son Bucky, who had recently filed for bankruptcy after reading *Art of the Deal* and needed a gig.

"Team, our careers have been inextricably intermingled, and as we reset our futures after this tragic watershed moment for our company, it is imperative that ERR LLC recognize your contributions in a tangible fashion. I, for one, have done a lot of soul searching and have come to realize that there are aspects of life more important than material gain. As a result, I plan to dedicate the rest of my professional life to loftier goals. Therefore, when we return to Dallas, I have instructed the company's Public Affairs Department to issue the following press announcement:

"It is with great regret that we announce that Boone Cartwright, our founder, chairman and CEO will be leaving the company to pursue other interests. Boone, in conjunction with the Faith in Our Future Fund, plans to create the Enron Ethics in Business Institute at Southern Methodist University (SMU), where Boone will serve as chairman and visionary business leader. Bucky Thigpen will be executive director. All of us at ERR LLC wish him well in this new endeavor."

"Oh my," exclaimed Brooke.

"Whatever you say boss," responded Ron.

"Damn this is big. This will shake up the company. Anymore dough in that fund?" remarked Montavious.

"Glad you asked, Montavious," quickly responded Boone. "As you know, loyalty has always been important to me, and there are no three people that have been more loyal than you, Brooke and Ron. In recognition of this loyalty and your years of service to the company, the board of the Faith in The Future Fund has appropriated very generous departure packages for each of you, with only one very minor condition, that you sign a Non-Disparagement Agreement to protect the company from adverse publicity."

"Where I come from, that is called buying silence," responded Montavious. "I imagine all hell is going to break loose when the stockholders find out we have bled this company dry. This package better be pretty good," he continued.

"I assure you they are. Beyond the ordinary corporate severance packages where those who have screwed up the most get a bundle of money, these include the purchase of specific ventures for each of you.

For instance, Ron, in line with your dynamic personality and independent nature, the fund proposes to purchase six closed J.C. Penney stores to convert into combination bowling alleys/coin laundries. In order to qualify as a minority business, your mother will be chair of the board, and you will be CEO working for her. The six locations will be strategically positioned in some of the most boring, downtrodden communities, assuring you that this new concept will be the most exciting thing in town.

Brooke, your talent is readily apparent and something the fund recognized must be capitalized on. You are uniquely qualified to serve a major underserved class. When was the last time attention was paid to Texas oil wives who have been historically taken for granted by the retailers of Houston and Dallas? Oppression is something that must be combatted in every socioeconomic group. It is incumbent on you, Brooke, to step into the fray to address this injustice. Therefore, the fund is proposing to create the Let Them Eat Cake personal shopping company to help wealthy Texas oil wives navigate the treacherous retail environment in search of high-end clothes, baubles and other goods totally out of reach of ordinary working people. You will be founder and chief shopper.

Finally, Montavious, your years of fighting for social justice makes you distinctively qualified to assume responsibility in the creation of public policy. Granted, it may require some flexibility in your core beliefs, but you have always had an open mind. This think tank will be dedicated to individual and constitutional rights and liberties devoid of affinity groups, multiculturalism, union coercion or identity politics. It will be called the You're on Your Own

American First Foundation and will be housed in the former offices of the John Birch Society in Oil City, Pennsylvania, just a short drive from our nation's capital. The concept is so exciting that it has already received offers of supplemental grants from the Koch brothers and the DeVos Family Fund. You will be ensconced as executive director with authority to recruit and assemble some of the great minds from the far right to create thought-provoking pieces such as:

"No need for minimum wage"

"The death penalty is for losers"

"Clean air and water are way overrated"

"Some groups of citizens need to be able to take a joke"

"QAnon and the deep state deserve mutual respect"

Montavious, these and other research documents will be transformative, and you and the America First Fund will become cultural icons."

Just about that time, the Falcon 900 landed and began taxiing to the private terminal at Dallas-Fort Worth International Airport. Waiting outside was Sumnter Pendegrass seated at a card table with a bulging briefcase. Ashley Cupcake in a pink Michael Kors outfit and Ron's mother with a peanut butter and banana sandwich, which was her little boy's favorite.

As they began to deboard, Montavious spoke up. "Boone all of this sounds right on, but when you cut through it all, what kind of green are we really talking about?"

"Great question, Montavious. The compensation package for each of you will be at least mid-six figures and, as usual in corporate America, you get paid whether you succeed or not. We call it a 'Yahoo Package,' which means you get an exorbitant salary, plus benefits and an obscene payout if you fail to accomplish any of your objectives."

"Where do we sign?" they all responded in unison.

"Stop by the card table where Mr. Pendegrass is seated, and it will only take a minute."

THIRTY-THREE

Sean awoke with a throbbing headache on the front stoop of the National Political Corruption Hall of Fame. Tough conditions under which to rev up a new business plan for the museum, but one was desperately needed. Luckily, just about the same time Sean was rousing, Paddy returned from the mini mart in town with two large cups of coffee secured after Sean had returned with nothing more than a pounding head.

"What the fuck happened to you?" inquired Paddy who was casually concerned with the well-being of his business partner.

"The last thing I remember was that huge trucker dude — Mongoose — was smashing my head with a half-filled Hamm's Beer can and calling me a deviate bastard."

"Were you doing weird shit?"

"I don't think so. It seemed perfectly natural to lunge at the topless Dutch broad in the coffee shop drive-through. I think it was my re-entry that was the problem."

"Well, whatever. Did you learn anything from what they are doing over there that can help us get this shit show up and running?"

"Actually, I did. Getting my head pounded by a beer can after checking out some gargantuan knockers reminded me of some sales advice from the founder of Hooters, who declared, 'If you can't sell tits and beer, you can't sell anything.' We need sex and booze to create some marketing excitement and a new name with a little more panache."

"Well, sex and booze are an integral part of political corruption, so that's easy, but what about the name?"

"How about 'Swampland?' Hell, we could franchise it with a location in every state capitol and the District of Columbia. We staff each location with retired NFL and NBA cheerleaders and let the local clientele of lobbyists and politicians provide real-time political corruption. Drinks and meals will be priced just under the legal gift limit for that state as cover for compliance, but multiple credit cards for each lobbyist will be kept on file to facilitate skirting the law and sharing the largesse among multiple clients. Lap dancing, pole dancing and other outrageous activity will be frowned upon, but private 'constituent discussion rooms' will be available at a nominal cost where in-depth public policy can be discussed with the cheerleader from the team of choice."

"Booze and a full bar?"

"Absolutely! Bartenders will be recruited from the local hearing loss center, so when deposed, they can with integrity unequivocally state, 'I heard nothing.' This will be a big selling point and allow for the normal interchange between lobbyist and politicians."

"I think we have a winner here, but now how do we get this up and running? I am thinking organization and financing."

"Easy. Here is the scam. We keep the museum here in Glenn as a shell with a non-profit status chaired by Senator VanValkenberg, which keeps government funds flowing out of the State Historical Preservation Trust. It also keeps the good senator on the public dole, and since his best buddy is the new chair of appropriations, we are all but guaranteed the funds will keep flowing for the foreseeable future. Next we set up a for-profit subsidiary called Swampland ostensibly to create auxiliary museums. In reality, we sell franchises too soon-to-be term-limited politicians with access to economic development funds who hide their ownership in limited liability companies controlled by friendly lobbyists. A foolproof business plan. Corruption that facilitates corruption necessitating a museum dedicated to corruption while you and I and the honorable senator skim the take off the top."

Armando and Rosa could not believe their good fortune. The terrorist attack and resultant publicity had created a tsunami of business beyond their wildest expectations. So much so that they invested in a high-speed printer for Dr. Violin to keep her cranking out prescriptions 24/7. The pirated Girl Scout logo and trademark had done wonders by creating an aura of respectability, allowing them to exceed their most optimistic marketing and sales expectations, but it was also fraught with risk. Simply put, it was only a matter of time before the Girl Scouts found out what they were doing and sued their ass. Time for a new plan.

"Armando, I have some big ideas for our company that will take us in a new more legit direction but still utilizing our core competencies," explained Rosa to a completely stoned and befuddled Armando.

"What do you mean core competencies?"

"Drugs, you idiot. That is what we know best. We are too big for this town. We need to go international, and I know just the place. Puerto Rico."

"Why Puerto Rico?"

"Shit, even though the island is dead ass broke, they will still give you anything you want as far as incentives if you just promise them some piddling numbers of new jobs. That is why all those big drug companies are down there with special tax deals. The beauty for us is that we can get all the bennies, be close to our hooch suppliers in South America and Mexico while doing business in a place with lax DEA enforcement. We just blend in as another member of big pharma gouging the public — another shining example of the free market at work."

"Well, what are we going to do that we are not already doing?"

"We morph into a medical food company which leaves us in an unregulated gray zone between a drug and a food. By the time the FDA/USDA/DEA figure out what to do with us, we will have cashed out and be living in the Cayman Islands."

"How does this work?"

"Well, we use Coca-Cola as our model. A little bit of coke in their original formula makes it the elixir of its day. They then wean out the coke but maintain its image as the happy drink. We do the same with our medical foods. We slowly lower the THC content to just below traceable levels, drop the Girl Scout logo, but replace it with a green trefoil which everyone thinks is the Girl Scouts anyways and then do a charitable marketing program with the National GSA in New York — say a penny a package for each box sold to GSA — which keeps the consumer totally befuddled. It also allows us to strong arm retailers for shelf space. We accuse them of misogyny on social media if they don't give us some space. Hell, remember the book *Radical Chic and Mau-Mauing the Flak Catchers* about playing off liberal guilt? Well, this is the marketing version. Any store that refuses us shelf space is anti-female, sexiest and an instrument of capitalist oppression. Foolproof!"

"What about Glenn?"

"We keep it as a shell company so we don't have to pay back the state all the benefits we received. All that clawback stuff was unfair to begin with. The more I think about it, maybe we designate it as our virtual world head-quarters with no employees and identify Puerto Rico as a manufacturing hub. That way we can milk both govern-ments simultaneously. God, I love free enterprise!"

Jack Hightower devised his escape plan while cruis-ing in the slipstream of the governor's convoy. A pathway to the Villages in Florida is what he was after, and Audrey was his meal ticket to a relaxing, blissful retirement.

Trucks and cars lined the road to the Glenn Coffee Shop, but with the aid of state troopers, Jack was able to use the shoulder to navigate to where Audrey was perform-ing on her apple crate. Fans blowing her skirt, red lipstick, blonde wig, she was the Marilyn everyone remembered and loved. Her show had become such a spectacle that the nearby Haven of Rest Nursing Home had delivered lawn chairs and residents had encamped in front of her for an afternoon of free entertainment and nostalgia.

Capturing this moment on his cell phone, Jack emailed the video to his former protégé, Randy Ledbetter, who was in charge of marketing for the auto train, which delivered people and cars from northern climates to Florida to be plucked like chickens by the tourism industry there.

"Randy how about this action? If you had her on the train, it would keep the bar car hopping for at least another hour or two. Talk about a profit center. This woman does a Marilyn act second to none, and I think I can deliver her if you can only provide a freebie trip to Florida for the two of us. I will even throw in a special performance of

'Marilyn rides the Chattanooga Choo Choo,' in which she mounts a toy train. Guaranteed to get a rise out of every old goat and inspiring blue hairs on board to try and duplicate her when they get home."

Randy quickly responded, "Jack, great to hear from you. It has been a long time, but from this I can see you have not lost your sense for talent. I agree this might be a winner, especially in light of all the complaints we have been receiving on the entertainment front. It seems like a full season of Mr. Ed, the talking horse television show reruns, just doesn't satisfy the clientele like it used to. If you can make the next train the day after tomorrow, you've got a deal. In advance, I will do a blast email to my AARP mailing list and also do a posting on the seniorsingles.com Facebook page. Are we a go?"

"Randy, you've got a deal. See you the day after tomorrow."

Now Jack needed to contact Merwyn Schlotsky at The Villages.

"Merwyn, look at the crowds this woman is creating. Traffic is backed up for miles. Now we find out she has been designated Senior Celebrity of the Month by the Auto Train. This is big. I think I can deliver her if you can confirm free accommodations and meals for two. In addition, as a plus just for you, I will authorize publicizing her arrival by train, which will create an aura of the Hollywood days of the past. Why, I can imagine an entourage of seniors with fedoras and double-breasted suits to meet her. The Villages will become a national sensation."

"Jack, I like it," responded Merwyn. "This will add pizzazz to a marketing strategy that over the past few months has been almost solely reliant on our tie-in with Preparation H. In the senior citizen world, this is up there with Celine Dion starting a show in Vegas. If you can deliver her, I guarantee the two of you a free year-round condo and a meal plan at Cracker Barrel on I-75. What do you think?"

"That cinches the deal. See you at the train station," responded Jack.

Now all Jack had to do was persuade Audrey, aka Marilyn, to take a car ride, a train ride and settle down in her new home in Florida.

"Marilyn — yo, Marilyn. Jack Hightower over here," screamed Jack as Marilyn gyrated before the assembled crowd.

"Oh, Jack, my darling," she cooed in response in her most breathless à la "Oh, Mr. President" fashion as the real Marilyn had done with President Kennedy. "Where have you been?"

"My dearest Marilyn, I have been negotiating with MGM your next celebrity appearance and have arranged for a private train along with a few of your admirers to take us to Florida, where you will be the headline act at a new resort. It is a place that is fast becoming the blue hair Vegas. It's called The Villages, and you will make what

Wayne Newton did for Las Vegas look like a warm-up act. We even have Geritol interested in becoming a national sponsor."

That was all Marilyn needed to hear. She coveted being in the spotlight, and the train ride reminded her of her honeymoon with Joe DiMaggio, where the buzz had been 'If the train is rock-in, don't come knocking.' Sure, Jack was not the reincarnation of the "Yankee clipper," but here the talent pool over the past few years had been limited, and if he could help her create a new Vegas and restore her career, why not?

"Okay, big boy, I am ready to roll. Where to?"

"Just wave goodbye to your fans, get off the apple crate, hop in the car and off we go to make entertainment history."

Sweet Jesus, thought Jack. I have hit the mother lode!

THIRTY-FOUR

Extra security was in order for the formal blessing of the water pipes and the Wave of the Future Church in Glenn. Coming just days after the terrorist attack, the media would be in a feeding frenzy with all the major outlets in attendance. Fox News was sending three blonde co-anchors, and CNN organized a panel of 15 experts to discuss how the blessing might affect climate change. *The Wall Street Journal* reported that trading in Andy Frain Rent-a-Cop futures had doubled before the opening bell in anticipation of the need for extra security and the announcement by the CEO that the former head of security at the U.S. diplomatic facility in Benghazi had been retained as a consultant. In addition, as a show of force, yellow tape was everywhere and a squadron of Vespas was on standby.

The governor was sweating profusely as he bounded down the steps of the mansion, realizing that the time had finally come to implement the "Sanford Plan" and his long-awaited personal Hegira was about to begin. His favorite movie had always been *The Great Escape,* and he envisioned himself as the political equivalent of Steve McQueen with the same derring-do as the actor on his motorcycle escaping from the Nazis. The prison he was escaping was Lansing, where fussbudgets nitpicked on issues of morality, fraud, competence and integrity. It had gotten to the point where it was nearly impossible to govern! The puritanical ethos rampant in the state capitol was made all the more intolerable by his soon-to-be indictment by the attorney general for a simple lap dance and a week of soulful reflection with the same young lady in Jamaica at the taxpayers' expense. He always prided himself as a man of action, and now it was time to act. His plan was simple. After the blessing in Glenn, he and Matilda would clandestinely head to the beach, where captain Clive Barnsley would be waiting with his duck boat, fully provisioned, for an overnight cruise to Racine, Wisconsin, and a new life. He had already negotiated a succession plan with the Attorney General Elliott Dodge, which provided for the Lieutenant Governor Theodious Adamowski to assume a six-figure position as chair of the state commission in charge of planning the next constitutional convention in 2050. A tenure, which would ensure he was totally vested in the state pension fund, would also allow the attorney general, who was next in line of succession, to become governor while dropping all charges against his predecessor, the Honorable Earl Baumgarten, so the electorate could "heal" while "refurbishing the Democratic ideals that make the state great."

Jack Hightower also knew his day had finally come. One more announcement ceremony, this one fittingly a blessing, with the lovely Audrey as eye candy draped over his arm and then a leisurely drive to the Auto Train, where he would begin his life as a kept man. Quiet coffee time each morning, followed by a leisurely walk in the local shopping mall, lunch on his veranda overlooking I-75 watching all those poor bastards headed north, a nap and then the early-bird special at Cracker Barrel for dinner. Maybe even followed by a nightcap at home while listening to his favorite song, "When I Die, Just Bury Me at Walmart (So My Wife Will Come Visit Me)." He couldn't imagine a finer life.

Red and Ingrid also knew this was the culmination of a dream. Maybe, just maybe, that glistening Corvette he had fixated on when first becoming part of the world of economic development would come to fruition. Ingrid would have a church to call her own and a place to practice her ministry. He would have cash flow to support a lifestyle of copious consumption devoid of any moral circumscriptions. In other words, a playboy as proselytized by his teenage hero Hugh Hefner. All of this made possible by a series of pipes, water and a church provided by the taxpayers involving no upfront investment by him in any way, shape or form. Couldn't get any sweeter than this.

The day that dreams would come true was finally here. The Lord had blessed this historic occasion with a magnificent day of temps in the mid-seventies, a slight breeze and a placid lake. All of Glenn and those from the surrounding environs had been invited and were expected to attend, partly out of patriotic pride. In fact, 1,000 American flag pins with "These colors don't run" had been disseminated by the local VFW, and flyers announcing "free food at the church blessing" that were passed out the week before by the local chapter of Weight Watchers had helped stoke patriotic fervor and attendance. Jaap and Berdenna planned to close early so she could look for a top for her Dutch maid barista outfit and Rosa and Armando expected a pre-event rush after which they would close to attend. Rumor had it that the governor would be in attendance and was to be accompanied by a "Lansing power broker." Jack Hightower, chairman of the MEDC, also would be coming with a woman named Audrey, who liked to be called Marilyn. Everybody who was anybody was planning on attending, which, by the way, was how Sean and Paddy rationalized their attendance as "constituent outreach" and eligible for per diem and mileage reimbursable by the state.

The importance of the event was underscored by the fact that it was going to be covered live by the Prosperity Gospel Channel, which was a subsidiary of the Jim and Tammy Faye Bakker Foundation. The channel preached that "the more you give, the more you got" and constantly scrolled 1-800-$$$-SOUL as a number to call to make your pledge to a phone bank in the Cayman Islands, manned 24-hours a day by retired Amish auto mechanics.

Governor Baumgarten whiled away his time in his motorcade speeding to Glenn checking his Instagram photos and listening to the country classic "I Keep Forgetting I Forgot About You." He had arranged to rendezvous with Matilda in front of the Glenn Apothecary, where she explained she needed to purchase a little "pick me up." Truth be told, she was completely exhausted after having been strung out for days on cannabis-infused Girl Scout S'mores and Pop-Tarts. What she needed was some amphetamines to keep her going and figured Dr. Violin might be the person to write her a prescription. After a 30-second explanation of her condition and the reasons for it, Dr. Violin diagnosed her malady as "Chronic Fatigue Collapse" brought on by "low blood sugar" and prescribed her a 12-pack of high potency amphetamines, which, according to the medical journals would be enough to keep an elephant awake for 30 days. Matilda popped two and was good to go.

Staging for the Wave of the Future Church dedication and blessing of the pipes was moving ahead smoothly. The crew of the Prosperity Gospel channel had borrowed a set from Game Day on ESPN and scheduled coverage to begin an hour before the actual event with a panel of religious experts to discuss "cash to converts," "off-shore banking and the IRS" and finally "Bitcoin in the new religious order." Multicultural diversity was to be showcased by a performance of the Holland Wooden Shoe Dancers to the tunes of Lawrence Welk's greatest hits. This would be a first on national TV. Security was modeled after the Super Bowl, with three security rings providing an impenetrable barrier. The outer barrier consisted of a series of A-frame wooden barriers with diversionary warnings of "pot holes ahead" and manned by the best Andy Frain had to offer. The middle circle was a series of Vespas parked sideways with their emergency flashers on, and the inner circle was a series of daunting flashing signs declaring "no drive zone" to intimidate anyone from driving too close. All of this on the ground was to be augmented by a newly recruited member of the Civil Air Patrol providing reconnaissance in a Piper Cub and towing a banner, courtesy of Allstate Insurance, with the warning, "Cause an accident and your insurance rates will go up."

Situated between the Game Day panel set and where the pipes entered the church, the focal point of the ceremony, were rows of white folding chairs borrowed from a local funeral home that specialized in after death baptisms. For their donation, the funeral home would get free holy water after the church was up and running. The first few rows were reserved for VIPs or anyone who had joined the Water Is Life Club at $100 per month. Since the service was to be at sunset and on national TV, studio lights were placed strategically to provide illumination for the event while highlighting the "Call 1-800-$$$-SOUL" banner adorning the church wall just above the pipes. It looked like it would be a glorious evening.

THIRTY-FIVE

Governor Baumgarten loved the trappings of power but none more than his motorcade of state trooper SUVs with sirens blaring and lights flashing. It made him feel potent, and this was especially important rolling into Glenn to meet Matilda and execute the "Sanford Plan." He ordered his escorts to put on the full display of lights and sirens.

Pulling up to the Glenn Apothecary, there sat Matilda on an iron bench with eyes bulging as if toothpicks were propping open her eyelids. She could have qualified as a finalist in an Adam Schiff lookalike contest. She had the look of a prairie dog popping out of a hole in the desert. Her two tabs of speed had clearly kicked in, and sleep would not be an issue for at least another 48 hours.

Everybody who was anybody within a 100-mile radius was planning on attending the blessing of the pipes. Patriotic fervor had been elevated by playing nonstop sequences of "Proud to Be an American" by Lee Greenwood and "Where the Stars and Stripes and Eagle

Fly" by Aaron Tippin from roving sound trucks selling "Born to Die" bumper stickers ever since the terrorist attack a few days ago. It was a badge of valor to attend the ceremony and not to be kowtowed by foreign operatives who had attacked the homeland here in Glenn.

In addition to the governor and Matilda, Jack and his guest, Armando and Rosa, Berdenna and the senator, Sean and Paddy would all be in attendance regaled by Shriners on mini-scooters and the South Haven High School German band. A large screen borrowed from a now-defunct drive-in movie complex was set up for a teleconference with Bogey and Skeeter from the studio of *America's Most Wanted* in New York City just moments before the blessing scheduled at exactly 8:32 p.m., which would coincide with sunset. Andy Frain ushers were strictly enforcing identification requirements of either a valid driver's license, a Costco membership card or a current electric bill with an address within the 100-mile zone of security. The outpouring of support was beyond everyone's wildest expectations causing the local Fox News affiliate to proclaim that the gathering was "the second largest group ever assembled, second only to the Trump inaugural."

This pomp and circumstance was fitting for the occasion. Governor Baumgarten and Matilda were seated in the front row along with Senator VanValkenberg and his wife Berdenna, who was wearing a newly purchased T-shirt inscribed "Welcome to the Grand Tetons." Sean and

Paddy were seated in the row behind the senator and his wife along with Jack Hightower and his lady friend in a red cocktail dress and white long gloves, who was incessantly humming "Diamonds Are a Girl's Best Friend." Armando and Rosa were positioned in the third row behind the Lansing Contingent, having secured this privileged seating by greasing the palms of the Andy Frain ushers with weed-filled chocolate chip cookies and 50% off coupons for any purchase over $5 at the Glenn Apothecary.

At exactly 8:16 p.m. to the tune of "Wade in the Water" sung by the Calvary AME Baptist Church youth ensemble, Ingrid began her march down the center aisle to where the pipe of life entered the church building. Wearing a green choir cassock and a miter and carrying an aspergillum to sprinkle holy water, she resembled a medieval bishop on a mission. The whole event was a made-for-TV spectacle. The pageantry was to culminate with the blessing of the pipes at precisely 8:32 p.m. with the sun setting and a red glow allowing her to exorcise spirits of Satan as floodlights clicked on highlighting the banner of the Prosperity Gospel and calling on all who believed to call 1-800-$$$-SOUL with any major credit card to get right with the Lord.

As all eyes were riveted on Ingrid and her grand entrance, a lone emaciated squirrel scampered among the chairs and finally alighted on Matilda's purse containing the 10 tabs of amphetamines and proceeded to devour the entire packet. The pharmacological impact of digesting enough speed to keep a rhino awake for a month was to totally energize the inherent aggression of the squirrel into full attack mode, prompting the crazed beast to ravenously gnaw on the main power line. It was 8:31 p.m. when the unhinged rodent contacted the copper wire causing a complete and total blackout and the resultant shock sent the beast airborne onto the miter on Ingrid's head.

Hysterical pandemonium ensued. Screams of Al Qaeda, ISIS and "We are being attacked by Canada" were heard as panicked participants trampled the Shriners and the Andy Frain ushers. The AME ensemble tried to bolster the throngs with a rendition of "Onward Christian Soldiers," but to no avail. In all the chaos, however, Governor Baumgarten kept a cool head. Although, Matilda was shrieking, "I will get you PETA bastards," he realized this was their moment and texted Captain Barnsley, "Time to waddle." The anticipation of Matilda and him being in a state of rapture in the pump room of the duck boat on the way to Wisconsin put him in a state of heightened excitement and profuse sweat.

Grabbing Matilda by her recycled hemp belt, he dragged her to the storage shed, where a 1994 Ski-Doo snowmobile had been left and might serve as a means of escape even though there was no snow.

Meanwhile, the sudden blackout of TV coverage resulted in thousands of ballistic viewers calling hundreds of local stations around the country concerned that another terrorist attack by "Godless foreigners" had occurred and seeking reassurance that *Days of Our Lives* would be shown as scheduled. The White House, trying to install calm in an election year, downplayed the incident by stating, "Since Michigan and the Midwest is flyover country, it appears as if the terrorist simply forgot to fly over." Two U.S. senators on a fact-finding mission with their confidential assistants in Aruba hastily organized a press conference in front of the Pink Pony Club to announce a bipartisan investigation into the media bias against Midwest values and the impact on national security. Finally, the Department of Homeland Security issued a code red alert elevating it from the previous yellow status. When advised by a 21-year-old cub reporter at an NBC affiliate in Waterloo, Iowa, that the color-coded system had been eliminated in 2011, the spokesperson defiantly responded, "Well, the American people get my drift." The nation was once again on high alert.

THIRTY-SIX

D isoriented by the crazed squirrel chewing copper wire now perched on her head, Ingrid's phantasm was that Glenn had become a modern-day Sodom and Gomorrah suffering the wrath of God. Just as described in the Bible in Exodus when total darkness befell Egypt for three days. Now Glenn for its evil transgressions was subject to total darkness. She knew her calling had come, and it was ordained that she lead the flock to the light whereupon she leaped up onto the snack table and perched between the fried elephant ears and the Twinkies, all the while with a nonplussed squirrel on her head, she delivered her sermon of salvation for Glenn. "This hellfire and brimstone is a direct result of the miscreant citizens we have gathered here in our town. Only help from the heavenly will rid us of this plague now before us and eliminate this den of inequity we now call Glenn." Her exhortation fell mainly on deaf ears as the crowd trampled one another seeking escape from what was undoubtedly another terrorist attack. It did resonate, however, with

Senator VanValkenberg. Heathen foreigners, a biblical plague and even an endangered squirrel as a sop to animal rights activists. This was too good to be true.

"Never let a serious crisis go to waste" was the sage advice of Rahm Emanuel, the former congressman, White House chief of staff and the mayor of Chicago. Senator VanValkenberg had great respect and admiration for anyone who could climb to the pinnacles of Illinois politics and not go to jail. Governor Rod Blagojevich had been his role model until he got sent to the slammer. Now, Rahm was someone to emulate.

After thoughtful evaluation of the situation for a nanosecond, the good senator understood his first responsibility was to find a live TV camera in front of which he could explain an occurrence about which he knew nothing. Facts were irrelevant at a time like this when demagoguery was in order. He could cite no less a biblical scholar than Rev. Johansson, pander to the fears of terrorism and appear caring by demanding that squirrels be put on the endangered species list. Now, where is that damn TV?

Armando and Rosa understood their first responsibility was self-preservation and outrunning the panicked throngs was the first order of business. They also understood there was money to be made by getting back to the store, where there would be a run for drugs to cope with anxiety, depression, PTSD and every variation of stress. All of which qualified for an exemption from the anti-price gouging laws, which became operational under a provision inserted by the pharmaceutical lobby in times of "war, insurrection, martial law, declared states of emergency or general chaos as determined by the local pharmacy." In other words, price gouging was legal in the very conditions when it should be illegal, as in these trying times. It was the patriotic duty of Armando and Rosa to open the store with significantly inflated prices and to join a long line of entrepreneurs exploiting a crisis for personal gain. It was the American way.

Sean and Paddy similarly felt a rush of patriotic fervor and actually for a very brief moment considered joining the National Guard. This notion was quickly discounted when they considered how they for years claimed "genetic, congenital bone spurs" as a way to avoid the draft, which might trigger legal issues of a criminal nature if now they were to miraculously disappear. After a few moments, a much more practical reaction kicked in involving how best to exploit the transformation of the National Political Corruption Hall of Fame — i.e., Swampland — into a nationwide franchise. Self-enrichment has always been part and parcel of national emergencies and why should this be any different? Cloaking the expansion as a patriotic endeavor would allow local franchises of "Swampland" to access local economic incentives as a free enterprise reaction to those who would challenge our way of life. It would also provide a nexus for expanding each facility to include an international lobbyist for arms manufacturers, telecommunications, spyware, Russian trolls and other exploiters of social media. In addition to the "Abramoff Bar" focused on domestic corruption, each Swampland would have a "national security chat room" with hookah pipes for rent individually or at a group rate, as well as a gift shop selling the latest in terrorist garb and xenophobic bumper stickers. Once this concept hits the newswires, it would immediately become a darling of Wall Street.

In the midst of all the chaos, Governor Baumgarten composed himself and realized this was the opportune moment to make a break for it. He commandeered a server's cart and flopped a befogged Matilda over the top and pushed her and the contraption over the field toward the shed where the getaway abandoned snowmobile was located. He was exhilarated by the thought that he soon would be immured with Matilda in the aptly named pump room of Captain Barnsley's duck boat headed for a life of promiscuous bliss in Wisconsin.

It was not lost on him that the server's cart now being used to transport Matilda was previously carrying pigs-in-a-blanket, which further heightened his mental stimulation already in a state of extreme desirousness. The physical exertion along with the mental titillation had him in such a state of sweating, he looked like someone just leaving a shower and looking for a towel.

Matilda had the look of a freshly caught fish flopping on the deck of a boat, especially when the cart hit a rut and she appeared to be executing some version of the Fosbury Flop. It took all of the governor's mass to keep the buggy rolling, but with his reward within reach, he was not to be deterred. All he had to do was make it to the shed, crank up the snowmobile, transverse the half mile to the beach where Captain Barnsley would be waiting and the Sanford Plan would be in full execution mode.

In the melee that followed the terrorist blackout, Berdenna's "Welcome to the Grand Teton's" shirt had been strategically ripped to obliterate the 'e,' leaving the 'T' on one side and 'tons' on the other with her cleavage creating a gulch in between. The former Dutch maiden now had the unmistakable look of a suggestive hooker as she scrambled to catch up with her husband who was in unadulterated high-gear political exploitation.

Senator VanValkenberg's uncanny instincts to find a camera were in full tracking mode. He was the human equivalent of a heat-seeking missile locked on a target. He knew whoever was first to get a national feed with a report of biblical connotations and terrorism as dual causations would immediately be invited to appear on Fox & Friends and with any luck, would be subject to the scorn of the Democrats' newsletter — i.e. *The New York Times*. Any attack by *The New York Times* always successfully enraged his base.

He calculated that the most likely place to find a television crew would be in front of the National Political Corruption Hall of Fame, since it would be a natural backdrop for any earnest young reporter. Sure enough, as he rounded the corner running at full throttle, parked in front was the Channel 88 Action News Roving Eye van with crack reporter 22-year-old Missy VanDijk. Missy had captured this coveted position after working three weeks as an intern when the entire newsroom quit after management disallowed any stories on Harvey Weinstein, declaring the #MeToo Movement was just fake news meant to destabilize the American workplace. Missy recognized the senator, having read "How Lansing Works," distributed by the capitol's sergeant of arms during her high school field trip and quickly deduced that an exclusive interview with him might be the big break she was looking for. Why on earth a half-topless woman wearing F-me pumps was in full pursuit of him was immaterial.

"Senator VanValkenberg, Missy VanDijk reporting with Channel 88 Action News. Can you tell our viewers what has happened?"

"Missy, I have just left the front lines where the battle of good vs. evil is underway. Two terrorist attacks in as many days proves that the town of Glenn has the sword of Damocles hanging over it, and I join Rev. Johansson in calling for its citizens to get right with the Almighty. As you know, I am a strong proponent of the separation of church and state, but under these circumstances, I will push through a supplemental appropriation to make sure the church is fully funded and operational."

Just as the senator made this headline-grabbing announcement, worthy of Wolf Blitzer invoking it in breathless tones as only he can do, the blonde big-bosomed woman in the ripped T-tons shirt lurched in front of the camera between the startled senator and Missy. Flummoxed after realizing where she was, but astute enough to realize this was her chance moment of fame, she screamed out, "God save us. The governor is missing."

The image of Berdenna and her pronouncement went viral. The reaction was immediate and widespread. Lieutenant Governor Theodious Adamowski, who was next in line of succession, issued a statement citing the "Israeli approach," declaring, "We will not pay ransom for his release. The governor would rather give his life than give in to terrorists. We all pray for his safe return, but I am prepared to serve if he doesn't." CNN immediately announced a "Breaking News" special with a panel of 22 experts to discuss "Executive Succession in an Age of Turmoil," while Fox News empowered an investigative team to examine whether "the deep state was behind the missing governor." Considering Berdenna and her 'T-tons' shirt was on every front page, it made sense that the teamsters invited her to be the keynote speaker at their annual convention, and ad campaign was commissioned by the Wyoming State Tourism Board calling on all U.S. citizens to "Come to Wyoming and See What You Are Missing — We Fill in the Missing 'E' With Excitement." The response to the ad campaign was so overwhelming that the website crashed and bookings for the Grand Teton National Park were suspended.

Sean and Paddy could not believe their luck. Live TV coverage outside the Hall of Fame was having just the impact they had hoped for. This was the perfect rebranding opportunity and a way to reach potential investors in a persuasive subliminal fashion. Soon cable reports, news affiliates and radio stations were all scurrying about trying to fill airtime by interviewing almost anybody, about anything, including Dr. Paddy Fitzpatrick, a now self-proclaimed Ph.D. in "political history and the interrelationship of terrorism and the need for government to make free enterprise work." He hastily purchased a tweed sports coat with elbow patches from the local Goodwill Store and issued an "availability" press announcement to discuss "the burgeoning movement for each state capital to establish a watering hole where historians, academics, legislators, lobbyists, fundraisers and working girls can all be recognized for their contributions to our system of government." Demand for his time was overwhelming.

Armando and Rosa watched all this unfolding next door and remembering a business book they had read entitled *Best Practices by Bernie Madoff,* issued a totally unsubstantiated tweet directed at Wall Street and the Puerto Rican Economic Development Commission about a pending "mutually synergistic alliance" between the Glenn Apothecary and Swampland. They went on in subsequent tweets to extol how "drugs and legislators are a natural fit" and that by combining "their core competencies, they will create a results-driven enterprise with a customer focus positioned for growth. It will also help eliminate climate change." This last reference was intended to make the proposed merger consistent with the goals and aspirations of the Business Roundtable.

To say the investment community was abuzz with the announcement was an understatement. Goldman Sachs issued an immediate invest recommendation citing this as the classic "How Do You Make Something from Nothing and a Harbinger of the Next Dot Com Era?" They discounted any concerns about management by claiming a bunch of trained monkeys could run this business and referenced all the corporate speak in the announcement as proof they knew what they were doing. *The Wall Street Journal* editorialized that the partnership "captivated the American entrepreneurial spirit, proving once again how government needs to get out of the way once they have provided sufficient corporate welfare to make it work." Finally, the National Bartenders Union announced an affiliation with the National Association for the Deaf to provide a steady stream of qualified bartenders to meet the expected demand and also to help fight climate change.

THIRTY-SEVEN

Seaman E-1 Finn Bjornstad was proud of his new position in the Coast Guard. He had always dreamed of a career as a seafarer and a life on the water after a summer job as a lifeguard at the community pool in Bowbells, North Dakota, where he grew up. He initially considered the Navy, but when he found out it didn't have a cool motto like the Coast Guard with Semper Paratus, he opted to see the world with them.

Stationed in Racine, Wisconsin, Finn was assigned to a top-secret project he had read about in the *Chicago Tribune*. It was an experimental warning system installed around the Great Lakes to predict "tidal waves," or so called "meteotsunamis." This multimillion dollar system was the product of an earmark in the Congressional Maritime Appropriations Bill placed by a local congressman whose boat was "jostled unnecessarily during cocktail hour," causing "trauma, concern and spillage." The intricate system was designed to detect any abnormal pressure on the water of the Great Lakes, which could result in massive waves disrupting "sunbathing, perch fishing, sunset cruises and possibly impacting liquor sales at beach front venues."

Seaman Bjornstad was quite proud of his position and responsibility on watch over the monitoring system from 11 p.m. to 7 a.m. He took it quite seriously but was also quite proud of his ability to multitask by simultaneously surfing the sailor dating website, anyportinastorm.com and its companion chat room fullmastatsea.com during the eight-hour shift. This night was no different. Calm winds, 0-1 foot waves and with a good weather forecast, he was excited to be able to continue his chat with Monique from France, who said she was now living in Racine, where she ran the Pleasure Palace Emporium, offering discounts for a full body massage to all members of the armed services protecting us night and day. Coincidentally, during their last chat, she had discussed that guys from North Dakota really turned her on.

Governor Baumgarten was suffering an acute case of erotomania for Matilda as he swung open the doors of the shed containing the snowmobile escape vehicle. The beating she had taken strapped over the server cart appeared to have revitalized Matilda to a state of semi-consciousness as she began to mumble expletives punctuated by the question, "What the fuck are we doing?" The governor, in an attempt to keep her calm explained, "Matilda, we are going on a vacation. Kind of a cruise. Just think of the Love Boat with a different crew and fewer staterooms."

This seemed to calm Matilda as she hummed the Love Boat theme song while watching the governor struggle to start the snowmobile. The battery was dead, so he repeatedly yanked on the pull start, building a sweat, which was excessive even for him. Finally, by putting all his weight behind one mighty pull, the snowmobile belched black smoke, sputtered and finally revved to life. It was just then that Matilda noticed the red and white consumer label warning label:

"Under no circumstances is this machine to be used without a helmet. To do so, is a violation of USC 18-SEC 22 and MI PL 499-18. Penalties may include up to 10 years in prison, $5,000 fine or both."

She let loose an ear-shattering shriek and then bellowed, "I can't ride that thing without a helmet. As a consumer advocate, I have spent my life imposing universally ignored warning labels to the public. My status as a national nanny would suffer irreparable harm. I am not getting on that thing."

An aghast governor responded, "Have you lost your befuddled brain? This is our way to the Love Boat and Xanadu."

"I am not getting on that thing."

Holy shit, he thought. I have a total whack job on my hands and were it not for his overwhelming concupiscence for Matilda and getting her to the pump room, he would abandon her right now.

Calculating his next move, he spotted a 1966 John Deere Model 60 lawnmower with what looked to be about an eight cubic foot dump cart in tow. The only warning label cautioned *"To discard trash responsibly."* He had a Plan B.

"Matilda, squash into this dump cart to create an energy saving air flow. Less friction, less energy used and you will be doing your part as a conservationist to attack global warming," all of which made perfect sense to the pixilated consumer zealot while tugging on her progressive heart strings.

Starting the dilapidated contraption would once again require his garnering all his mass as he stomped on the kick starter repeatedly hoping to get some kind of reaction from the machine. His lust for Matilda was such that whatever exertion it took to get it started was not going to deter him. In fact, pumping the pedal just served to remind and excite him as to what was ahead. Finally, the engine coughed, followed by a blast of soot and smoke harking success. Regretfully, the unmuffled engine had covered Matilda with a black film, making her look like a scarecrow in blackface. Oblivious to her new look, Governor Baumgartner excitedly yelled out, "Hold on, hot pants, we are going for a ride," whereupon he twisted the handlebar accelerator to full throttle, lurched out of the shed and across the rutted field while Matilda flopped like a rag doll, all while humming the *Love Boat* theme song once again.

Captain Barnsley had beached the duck boat at the appointed spot and was patiently waiting for his two intrepid passengers. The weather and waves were both forecast to be calm, so he anticipated a smooth and uneventful cruise to Racine. Per the governor's orders, the pump room was to be stocked and provisioned as the love nest. Two lava lamps were strategically placed at each end of the berth and a boom box with a CD of Wayne Newton's *Greatest Hits* was ready to play at the tap of a button. In addition, two iced bottles of Boone Farms Apple Wine with champagne flutes and an ample supply of Cheetos, Doritos and Pop-Tarts would provide sustenance during the romantic journey.

Before vaulting from the shed and mounting the John Deere, the governor realized that a mere handkerchief would not suffice in mopping his sweat. Luckily, he spotted a container of red checkered handyman big wipes on the back shelf and inserted two in each armpit, one around his neck as a bandanna and another on top of his head as a durag. Now in command of the John Deere escape vehicle and exceeding speeds of 8 mph, he appeared to be a bulbous Yasar Arafat lookalike, further stoking rumors of a terrorist attack. Reports of an Aladdin type character with a tablecloth on his head stoked the Glenn community already rife with rumors. The reported sighting of a Middle Eastern-appearing individual escaping triggered news alerts around the nation and confirmed the event was a terrorist attack.

After a 15-minute trek over the abandoned field, they reached the cliff overlooking the beach and the duck boat. Matilda's brain was totally addled by the jarring ride. The governor, exhausted but driven by surging levels of testosterone, detached the dump cart and with a mighty surge sent it, with Matilda, cascading down the cliff until it hit an evergreen stump, halting further progress but launching her the final 10 feet. She landed unceremoniously, spread eagle in front of Captain Barnsley. Meanwhile, the governor contemplating the 96 steps to the beach decided to try and drive the John Deere mower down the cliff, resulting in the machine doing a series of forward somersaults and finally coming to rest a few feet from the caterwauling Matilda. It was an ugly scene.

The governor with his durag askew staggered to his feet and motioned to Captain Barnsley to help him grab Matilda by her ankles. Dragging her up on the ramp spread eagle, they managed to reach the pump room door, whereupon they shoved her head first into the compartment. The governor squeezed his way through the hatch, lumbered down the steps, pushed the comatose Matilda to the side and, lying prone on the floor, tried to regain his strength by devouring a six-pack of chocolate-frosted Pop-Tarts.

Captain Barnsley loved the serenity of a nighttime cruise. Placid waters, stars overhead and a steady hum of the engines made all copacetic with the world, and tonight was no different. It was strangely quiet in the pump room until quietness was broken by loud and abrupt "thump."

The long-experienced captain assumed it was the passion of Governor Baumgarten and Matilda and reminded him of that old rule of the sea, "Every man finds a port in a storm," so he continued to sail ahead.

Down below, the loud "thumps" and their increased frequency began to rouse Matilda. The governor was oblivious to the sound, preferring to concentrate on the Cheetos now that he had finished the Pop-Tarts. However, despite his being unmindful of the cacophony of "thump," "thump," "thump," it was alarming Captain Barnsley and especially when a 15 lb. fish, followed by another of equal size, flew over the transom at eye level. These two were followed by three more "flying fish" hurdling over the bow. Soon it was a feeding frenzy of massive airborne fish flying every which way over the boat. They were not salmon, walleye or trout but some kind of species unfamiliar to the captain. Then it struck him. OMG, these were the dreaded Asian carp that had been working their way up the Mississippi River and threatening to destabilize the entire Great Lakes ecosystem. Somehow this school of fish had circumvented the electronic barriers in Chicago and now were loose in Lake Michigan. The captain and his duck boat were dead center of this ecological catastrophe.

The incessant banging was quite irritating to Matilda as it stirred her from her stupor. Looking across the pump room at the clueless governor chomping on Cheetos and totally oblivious to the sounds further annoyed her. It was only after she heard Captain Barnsley scream out "Sweet

Jesus" that she barked at the governor, "Get your fat ass up there and do something," rousting him from junk food nirvana. Terrified of her wrath, he lumbered up the steps, opened the hatch and stepped up on the back deck.

Seaman Finn Bjornstad was thoroughly enjoying his chat with Monique on the fullmastatsea.com website. He was so captivated by her that she was able to persuade him to upgrade his status to platinum by buying access to the "Maiden of the Sea" section where "the girls bare all and share their most intimate desires." Luckily, the lust for Monique coincided with a totally blank meteotsunami screen, allowing him to focus all his attention on her and her professed craving for North Dakota studs. Fortunately, the Maiden of the Sea private room was made affordable by the six $10 debit cards he had pilfered from his grandmother as part of her 'Quilts R Us' frequent sewer awards program. The pin number was her birthday.

Monique had just responded how excited she was to have him join her in the 'Exclusive Den of Carnal Desires,' when a yellow alert light on the early warning meteotsunami system began to blink. Focusing on the task at hand, Finn disregarded the light as a simple system malfunction and entered another debit card just seconds before his exclusive rendezvous with Monique was about to be timed out.

Damn it, thought Finn. How inopportune as the red emergency light and siren kicked into gear indicating a major tsunami event with catastrophic waves and currents.

He still had eight minutes left of his private chat with Monique, and it was a precious time not to be wasted on an errant alert.

Unbeknownst to Finn, Governor Baumgarten finally standing erect on the back deck of the boat had been gobsmacked in the head by two 18 lb. flying Asian carp. Captain Barnsley was hiding under the pilot house screaming mayday into the ship-to-shore radio when he heard the governor bellow out, "Jesus Christ." Turns out the two crazed massive carps that had hit the governor in the head, caused him to catapult over the starboard side directly into the school of fish swarming around the boat. It was a case of shock and awe. The massive girth of the governor hitting the water caused such displacement that it triggered the meteotsunami warning system 40 miles away in Racine. It also had what was to become known as the "depth charge" effect by stunning the entire school of invasive carp into a listless floating mass of dead fish. Governor Earl Baumgarten of Michigan had saved the entire Great Lakes, 20% of the fresh water in the world, from an ecological disaster of an invasive species.

THIRTY-EIGHT

G lenn had become a national rallying cry in the war against evil, terrorism and all those who would endanger the free enterprise system. The second incident in the small Michigan town unleashed a xenophobic feeding frenzy in Washington, D.C. A bipartisan group of senators introduced legislation to build a moat between the U.S. and Canada to protect our "Northern flank" to be paid for by an excise tax on the income of Celine Dion who, as a Canadian, had made "windfall" profits in the USA. As further justification, the conservative Republican Freedom Caucus invoked Barry Goldwater when he said, "Extremism in defense of liberty is no vice" and the Democrat Progressive Wing cited the need to keep North Dakota and Minnesota cool in the face of powerful worldwide warming trends.

Another group of legislators prodded by the Club for Growth and the Socialist Worker's Party proposed legislation that would nationalize economic incentives as a means to keep the free enterprise system "robust and healthy," while the Christian Coalition in conjunction with the Islamic Circle of North America and Jewish Federation supported "a federal matching grants program for all tax deductible contributions made to religious institutions as a means to keep God in our lives."

As the country sat glued to the television watching events unfold in the tiny Midwest town on Lake Michigan, Elaine Cabot Swarthmore struggled to capture a concept for her Harvard MBA business dissertation on philanthropic investments. She had been admitted to the exclusive program after referencing on her application her dedication to "tearing down the financial and cultural barriers preventing the historically disadvantaged from economic class advancement." Her acceptance was made under a special program administered by the dean to ensure openness and diversity of thought, and it was noted that her acceptance had no relationship to the $100 million donation her father, Edwin Cabot Swarthmore IV, had made to the university Keep Our Legacy Alive fund.

Sitting on the floor of the Worker-Student Alliance Office pondering her thesis, Elaine caught out of the corner of her eye Lou Dobbs of Fox Business News interviewing Armando, Rosa, Sean and Paddy. This famous host was exploring the notion that capitalism was the main deterrent to second-generation immigration terrorism. This line of questioning allowed Paddy and Sean to wax eloquently on how it was to grow up under the scourge of the potato famine and how they were now banding with their Cuban brother and sister to reap the fruits of capitalism. Armando and Rosa seized the moment to interject how two Cubans partnering with the Irish duo was a "synergistic, all-in approach, using their limited bandwidth to go live with their bizmeth." No one, including Elaine, had any idea of what they were talking about, but the jargon was persuasive. She quickly researched the business plan of the joint venture on their Facebook page and when she discovered it had over a 100 likes was convinced of its viability. She quickly sketched out a feasibility piece on her iPad on the concept of a national franchise called Swampland with a presence in every state capital and the District of Columbia. She went on to support the combination of drugs and political corruption as fundamentally sound and supported by empirical data. In addition, growth opportunities included such potential subsidiaries as "One Not Enough Drug and Alcohol Treatment Centers" as well as "Never to Return Bail Bonds." She went on to comment that by combining Cuban and Irish ownership, the fledgling entity would qualify for every do-good grant, credit and incentive the government was doling out, while allowing politicians to ingratiate themselves with two key constituencies. In a nutshell, this is what philanthropic investment was all about — making money in the guise of social welfare.

Elaine knew she was onto something and quickly drafted a cover note for the synopsis and emailed it to her daddy's admin requesting that she type, spell check, format, proofread and verify the numbers for submission to her professor. It also occurred to her that since her father was the senior partner and chief officer of the Goldman Sachs Philanthropic Fund, he might see this as a way for his little girl to acquire a position in this dynamic new corporate entity.

Mysteriously, after the admin had made 100 copies of Elaine's report for the Goldman Sachs Philanthropy Executive Committee, word of the pending proposal somehow appeared in the "Heard on the Street" column in *The Wall Street Journal*, written by the admin's second cousin. This leaked information immediately started a buzz in the investment community that Swampland was a sure-fire bet and that anybody left on the sidelines would regret the day. The article also caught the attention of the Puerto Rico Economic Development Commission, which immediately began to create a far-reaching incentive package, including zero taxes on all executive salaries and free country club memberships to all officers of the company, to insure that the commonwealth would be designated the drug manufacturing hub of this soon-to-be national franchise.

While Swampland was the talk of Wall Street, Senator Jaap Vanderveen and Berdenna were speeding their way back to Lansing with a state trooper escort they had commandeered in Glenn. Although the senator would be out of office in a few days, he still chaired the Appropriations Subcommittee on Economic Development, and the crisis in Glenn provided an opportunity to jam through an emergency supplemental appropriations bill loaded with pork for the faith-based community, Dutch entrepreneurs and all his other favorite constituencies. His most favorite being himself.

The first order of business was some new attire for Berdenna, but the only place open was a beach shop where they settled on an XXL T-shirt proclaiming, "Come Play with Me" over an outline of Lake Michigan. They also invested in some flip-flops to replace the F-me pumps in anticipation of a highly publicized meeting with the lieutenant governor being billed as a behind-the-scenes look at your government in action.

The Lieutenant Governor Theodious Adamowski knew this was his moment to look decisive as he grabbed the reins of power. Prior to being picked to join the ticket with Governor Baumgarten, he had been the chief ethics officer of the Teamsters Union Central States Pension Fund. How he handled himself in this crisis would be the defining moment of his nascent political career. The optics of this were more important than the substance. He would need to appear firm, caring and compassionate, which meant the usual array of sycophants lining the executive board room as he and Senator VanValkenberg pretended to haggle over the predetermined amount and scope of the emergency supplemental appropriations.

Smelling money, lobbyists were swarming the halls. The true worth of a lobbyist was how successful they could be in getting their clients included when they had absolutely no bearing on the issue or problem to be solved. The so-called Christmas tree effect was in full force with the emergency supplemental — $350,000 to determine whether daylight savings affects the drive-in movie business, $1.2 million to study the impact of mandatory unionization on organized labor, $2.3 million to examine the impact of cow flatulence on climate change and two items of special importance to Glenn: $4.2 million for faith-based aerial deterrence of terrorism along with $3.3 million for a caffeine-based rest stop for truckers within a two-mile radius of the recent terrorist attack.

The entire legislative package was rushed through in a midnight session under a parliamentary process called suspension of the rules, which meant no roll call vote providing plausible deniability for any legislator wanting to disavow responsibility. With Governor Baumgarten MIA, the lieutenant governor's late night signing ceremony as acting governor coincided perfectly with his first big fundraiser hosted that same day by the Coalition for Responsible Government and Fiscal Integrity.

Red knew a good thing when he saw it. Selling bottled holy water to tourists was lucrative, but wholesale aerial spraying was in a whole other league. Slipping the funding into the supplemental appropriations bill now made his plan feasible. Pump water from Lake Michigan, have it blessed by his wife, the bishop, and then spray it from crop dusters as a deterrent to the godless foreign terrorists.

Now, paying for the holy water might appear unseemly, so just tuck almost all of the $4.2 million under administrative expenses/overhead. All he had to do now was find a couple of good ol' boys to do some heavenly spraying.

The Jackson boys, Keith and Kevin, supplemented their unemployment checks with cash-only sightseeing rides for tourists in their vintage Stearman Model 75 open cockpit airplane. Dressed in leather helmets and aviation goggles, they promised a true barnstorming experience. They had been in the crop dusting business, but were ordered to cease and desist by the Environmental Protection Agency (EPA) after they were found to be spraying outlawed DDT as a cost-cutting measure. Although active in the "Get Government Off Our Backs" movement, when approached by Red to spray holy water at a government funded $1,000 an hour, a fee split evenly between Red and the two of them, they considered it their moral and civic duty to lend their God-given talents to the cause.

The process was rather simple. Water pumped from Lake Michigan was routed through the Wave of the Future Church, where it was blessed three times a day by the Bishop Ingrid Johansen. These "sanctification and purification ceremonies" were open to the public for a nominal contribution of $10 per person. Following the ceremony, the water was transported to the Jackson brothers' aerial circus hangar in a converted street-sweeping truck, where it was funneled into the 400-gallon holding tanks of each plane. Two flights a day, one at sunrise and the other at sunset, involved both planes with Keith and Kevin in full aviator regalia, accompanied by Bishop Ingrid with her miter and staff in the back passenger seat. Oftentimes, they would also include a photographer from the Aircraft Owners and Pilots Association (AOPA), who was writing a cover story for their member magazine entitled "The Importance of Private Aircraft in Carrying Out the Mission of God and Government."

Meanwhile, back on Wall Street the "Heard on the Street" column in *The Wall Street Journal* was resonating in the financial world. Kai Ryssdal of *Marketplace* on NPR intoned that the Goldman Sachs investment in Swampland could become the next darling of small cap investors. Neil Cavuto of Fox Business declared that Swampland would be to legislation what McDonald's was to hamburgers and Jim Cramer of *Mad Money* just screamed "Buy, Buy, Buy." All of this media hype excited the lemmings of the investment world into a state of deliriousness reminiscent of the dot.com bubble.

All of this financial attention was not lost on the Puerto Rican Economic Development Commission as they put together a "package" for Swampland. An abandoned Sears store was offered as a manufacturing site, all taxes waived and each executive would receive a complete set of Ping golf clubs and a dozen Pro V1 golf balls in addition to the free country club membership. In announcing the proposal, the Governor of Puerto Rico boasted that the "Commonwealth will never be outbid. and we will always

be competitive with Bangladesh, Vietnam and Senegal."
Armando, Rosa, Paddy and Sean were awash in cash.

Jaap and Berdenna quickly reconnoitered after the
$3.3 million windfall in the supplemental appropriations
bill. Berdenna recognized this cash infusion as an opportunity to rebrand the enterprise and make the most of its
distinguishing asset. The new entity would be called
Twin Peaks Rest Emporium and billed as a "haven for
truckers combating the solitude of the road with hot coffee
and even hotter baristas." They immediately acquired
a deserted Toys "R" Us with easy off and on to the interstate and "discrete" parking in the rear. In order to assure
diversity, they hired the entire staff of the now-defunct
Tokyo Massage chain of health clubs. Jaap, it was decided,
would continue as a silent partner with a six-figure
consulting contract to advise on community outreach. The
business would qualify as a minority-female-controlled
enterprise eligible for set-aside contracting preferences
with Berdenna as chair and CEO and Audrey Richenberg
of the Villages, Florida, as secretary and treasurer. News
of this new formidable competitor caused Starbucks stock
to drop precipitously.

As Swampland and Twin Peaks vaulted from obscu-
rity to the talk of Merrill Lynch and Morgan Stanley, the
Wave of the Future Church became a viral phenom. The
Bishop Ingrid Johansen in a biplane fighting the evil of
terrorism graced the cover of *People* magazine, *The
National Enquirer,* and *Flying Magazine,* characterized

her activities in Churchillian terms by declaring that "never has one done so much for so many." The coverage reached a crescendo when her exploits were the subject of a half-hour discussion on *The View.*

Her twice a day flight began to attract hundreds of gawking, admiring onlookers and a ready market for every manner of tchotchke, gewgaw and trinket extolling the saintly bishop. Swarms of vendors converged at each flight, more than happy to pay a royalty on each article sold. All this commotion was not lost on Hollywood, with Disney proposing a made-for-TV movie, "Ingrid Our American Joan of Arc."

Red was closing in on that brand new Corvette.

THIRTY-NINE

T alk about inopportune timing. Finn Bjornstad still had three minutes left on his platinum level access to the Maiden of the Sea website, and all of a sudden the meteotsunami monitor board red lights started flashing and the alert siren began screeching. All this just as Monique began to bare all and was suggesting that for a mere $10 upgrade, he could enter her den of desire where every man experiences nirvana.

Just as he was about to log in with another of his grandmother's $10 Quilts R Us debit cards, the code red hotline rang indicating a mayday distress call. Annoyed by yet another interruption, Finn decided what the hell, I guess I better answer it.

"Seaman Bjornstad here."

"Seaman, this is base commander, Captain Johrvon. We have received a mayday from a vessel on Lake Michigan, 42 miles due east of Racine and we need to dispatch rescue aircraft immediately."

"Yes, sir, captain."

Apologizing to Monique for the rude interruption, he radioed a twin engine Sikorsky MH-6 Jayhawk helicopter on routine patrol about a possible rescue at sea operation. The pilot, Lt. Commander Homer Dalrymple, and his co-pilot, Lt. Morris Fishback, immediately executed a sharp left turn and headed due east at a 1,000 feet to intercept the distressed vessel.

Streaking across the lake, they quickly encountered a duck boat adrift and a scene unlike either of the two experienced pilots had ever seen. The boat was surrounded by dead fish, and in the middle of this carnage was some sort of manatee type beast wearing a durag. There were hundreds of dead fish of a variety they had never seen and even more perplexing was that the beast with the durag clearly could not be a manatee, since they are not present in Lake Michigan. The chaos of the entire scene was compounded by the presence of a scarecrow-looking woman in blackface screaming at the top of her lungs, "Save the governor." The only reaction from Lieutenant Commander Dalrymple and Lieutenant Fishback was in unison, "What the fuck!"

The first order of business was to lower the rescue basket with crew member Seaman Jackson Jones with a grappling hook to pull in whatever the beast was behind the vessel. To the amazement of the young sailor, it was not any type of fish at all but rather a bulbous body emitting sounds like a beached whale. The sheer mass of the body made the basket inadequate, requiring some ingenuity by Seaman Jones. Spotting a sled usually reserved for ice water rescue, he pushed it toward the bovine body and using the grappling hook prodded the floating blob onto the sled, which he then tied to the stern of the boat to be towed in. He then grabbed a couple of dead fish and was hoisted back into the helicopter.

As soon as he was back, he dreaded what he knew he had to do next. The shrieking woman on the boat was in a state of cataclysmic meltdown. Her wailing was indecipherable and her continuous flapping of her arms made her look like a crazed stork unable to launch. Re-entering the basket, Seaman Jones lowered himself to the deck of the duck boat to retrieve the hysterical woman. Upon his arrival, Matilda leapt upon him by flinging her arms around his neck and her legs around his torso. She was totally latched onto him, all the while screeching, "Save the governor."

Just then a dazed Captain Barnsley squirmed out from underneath the pilot house scaring the bejesus out of Seaman Jones, who was locked in the embrace of Matilda. Thinking that Matilda had been the only person aboard, he bellowed out,

"Who the hell are you?"

"Clive Barnsley, captain of this ship. U.S. Navy, retired.

"Who are these people and where were you going?

"Governor Earl Baumgarten of Michigan and Matilda Hoffenmeister, Executive Director of the Coalition of

Concerned Citizens for Transparency and Ethics in Government. We are on a top-secret national security mission to Racine, Wisconsin."

"Well, where the hell is the governor then?"

To which Captain Barnsley responded by pointing at the blob of humanity on the sled behind the boat.

"Holy shit," exclaimed Seaman Jones. "We've gotta get out of here. Help me with this wild woman."

He then, with the assistance of Captain Barnsley, grabbed a couple of bungee cords, which he used to tie Matilda's feet and hands, whereupon the two of them unceremoniously tossed her into the basket. Once she was lifted and deposited into the belly of the helicopter, the basket was returned to the deck of the duck boat where Captain Barnsley clamored on board after declaring his boat was inoperable and in need of a tow.

Once Matilda, Captain Barnsley and Seaman Jones were safely ensconced in the Sikorsky rescue helicopter, Lt. Commander Dalrymple radioed back to Seaman Bjornstad that he was headed to the port of Racine and that the distressed vessel was abandoned and that it would need a tow and, oh by the way, "There is some guy they keep referring to as the governor on a sled behind the boat."

During the flight to Racine, the rattled Captain Clive Barnsley began to realize this entire fiasco jeopardized his $1.1 million subsidy under the Maritime Security Program, unless he could demonstrate how this cruise was undertaken with a "national security purpose." He was going to need to concoct quite a story that made this escapade, something quite different than simply a tryst between a lustful politician and his paramour. It was then that Matilda mumbled, "At least he saved us from those damn fish." That was all Clive needed to hear. He had a plan.

Seaman Bjonsky had just returned to Monique's website having qualified for elite platinum access when the order came to dispatch a cutter to tow in the duck boat. Although, once again irritated by the interruption, duty called so he put the site on pause and, using the Coast Guard ship-to-shore radio system, contacted a RB-S boat on routine patrol and hurriedly messaged as follows:

"Duck boat 42 miles due east of Racine needs tow. Passengers and crew being helicoptered back to the port of Racine. Please note, pulling governor on sled behind the boat. Over and out."

This transmission was picked up by the night beat reporter of the *Racine Journal* on his Maritime radio scanner. This reporter, Diether Klum, was not the brightest bulb in the closet, but even he figured out this story might be big. Like Pulitzer prize big, but he needed to own it and exploit it, so he sent out a PR wire news alert, "Heroics and the Governor. Exclusive interview on the Racine docks 8 a.m. this morning."

Now, he had no idea if anything heroic had happened and, if so, by whom, but those were just details he could worry about later. This was national news, that could catapult him into a position as a talking head on cable news or at a minimum being interviewed by Sean Hannity.

The RB-S cautiously approached the drifting duck boat pulling what at first glance by the captain appeared to be an inverted manatee rather than the governor. Upon further inspection, they were able to confirm no passengers or crew on board and that the mass on top of the rescue sled was actually a whale-shaped human being, which, given its size, presented the captain with a conundrum. Try and board the body or leave it on the sled as they towed in the vessel? Harking back to his Boy Scout merit badge on medical emergencies, he remembered the scout master's admonition to always leave someone prone until help arrived. Captain Franz Kohler, as someone who always followed the rules, determined it would be best to leave the gasping, snorting body on the sled instead of endangering his crew by trying to lift him aboard. They proceeded to hook the tow bar to the front of the duck boat with the sled attached to the stern and began the trek to the port of Racine.

Clive Barnsley and Matilda Hoffenmeister had been airlifted to the port of Racine, where a swarm of reporters had already gathered to wait for the arrival of the duck boat. Clearly this rescue mission had garnered a degree of national and international attention never experienced in Racine before. All of this attention further convinced Clive Barnsley it would cause an examination of the lucrative Maritime Security Incentive Package he had been milking at the taxpayers' expense. He needed to gin up a story as to what the three of them were doing last night and how it had national security connotations.

By 8 a.m. the Racine docks were a media circus. CNN had sent Chad Myers, its top meteorologist, along with six professors from the University of Wisconsin to discuss how climate change had affected lake levels and the ability of the Coast Guard to execute rescue missions. Fox News marshalled six blonde female experts to dissect how illegal immigration had adversely affected Coast Guard readiness by diverting resources to the Mexican border. Even Telemundo had sent reporters to emphasize the need for bilingual crew on every ship. It was a scrum of reporters, but during this melee, crack reporter Diether Klug had strategically positioned himself with three lawn chairs at the end of the pier to induce Clive and Matilda to join him to discuss what was being billed on streamers on cable channels as "Surviving the night of terror." Now all he had to do was wait.

Finally, as dawn began to break, the throng of the docks could make out the silhouette of a RB-S Coast Guard boat towing not one but two vessels. The appearance of the boats caused Matilda, who had now joined Diether and Clive at the end of the pier, to shriek out, "The governor is alive."

"What governor?" yelled a reporter from the back.

"Governor Baumgarten."

Bedlam ensued. Reporters and camera crews trampled one another to get the first photo/video or better yet interview the semi-conscious blob now identified as the governor of Michigan. All the jockeying by the media would be to no avail since Diether Klug had already strategically staked out the prime position. Not only did he have Clive and Matilda with him, but since the sled was behind the distressed vessel, it would be retrieved at the end of the dock where they were seated.

Sure enough, as Captain Kohler entered the port of Racine, he swung the duck boat abreast of the pier, followed by the sled with a now recognizable belching and convulsing Governor Earl Baumgarten. Upon his arrival and in recognition of the size of the load, three longshoremen with a boat lift were dispatched to the end of the pier to pluck him, while still on the sled, out of the water. All of this under the glare of TV lights and cameras.

Clive realized that if he was going to save his participation in the cash cow known as the Maritime Security Program, he was going to have to spin some wild story, so why not begin now? Standing before a bank of microphones and cameras, Captain Clive Barnsley, whom the world was now addressing as admiral, with the aplomb and chutzpah of a Trump press secretary declared:

"The world owes this man a debt of gratitude. He without fear or trepidation risked his life to prevent an environmental catastrophe. Confronted with an onslaught of Asian carp that would have permanently altered the ecosystem of 20% of the fresh water in the world and seriously impacting national security and world peace, Governor Earl Baumgarten sacrificed his body to protect us all. By launching himself into the water, he became a human concussion bomb, killing all the would-be invaders. He is a national treasure."

The media simply went berserk. Pictures of the prone governor on the sled of the pier periodically snorting and spasmodically jerking filled the airwaves and became a viral sensation on social media. Fox News claimed that he was better than a wall in stopping unwanted migration. CNN formed a panel to discuss "Historic moments in the environmental defense of our nation" and the Huffington Post categorized his activities as "raw political courage not seen since Mr. Smith went to Washington."

Matilda continued to observe in her fugue state brought upon by the trauma of the events while Captain Barnsley portrayed their crossing of Lake Michigan on par with D-Day. He explained how the three of them were united in doing whatever it took to defend the Great Lakes. He would captain the boat on a search and destroy mission. Matilda would serve as a scout in blackface so as not be seen by the enemy, and the governor was willing to put the full weight of his office behind stopping the invading carp.

The captain went on to recount that, much like a team of Navy SEALs, they searched for the enemy and clandestinely approached the carp ready to do battle. When Matilda spotted the school of fish, she signaled him with two flaps of her arms, whereupon he cut the engine indicating to the governor that the fish were in range. The governor grabbed his cast net, and with a mighty throw tried to encompass the entire school. Despite his best effort, the sheer size of the school was too large for the net, and he realized extreme measures would be necessary since the escape of even one was unacceptable. It was then that he mounted the stern transom and yelled, "I will give my life if need be," as he executed a cannonball into the frenzied school of Asian carp. The impact was such that every fish was stunned to death.

FORTY

The Goldman Sachs Philanthropic Executive Committee was called to order by its Chairman Edwin Cabot Swarthmore IV. A pompous easterner, his arrogance was exceeded only by his lack of accomplishment in anything of substance. His wealth and position were derived from his one singular positive trait of having been born in the right gene pool. He, however, considered both his wealth and position as a right that came with the name Swarthmore, and he was determined to create a sinecure for his daughter Elaine so she could carry on the family tradition.

The committee quickly approved a $10 million investment in Swampland. None of the members of the committee cared or understood the business plan, but the original agenda instructed them to vote yes based upon the progressive buzz words in the application that would make them look like leaders in the newly fashionable world of impact investing. The press release announcing the investment explained that Swampland would enable "minoritized" communities to obtain "economic justice" in an "inclusive" and "diversified" work environment devoid of "privilege." It went on in a footnote to mention that the Goldman Sachs Fund would be represented in the company by a recent Harvard Business School graduate serving in a paid advisory role with no operational responsibility. In other words, daddy's little girl, Elaine Cabot Swarthmore, would be on the company payroll to do nothing.

Now with a cool $10 million cash in the bank, Armando, Rosa, Sean and Paddy were the darlings of Wall Street and ready to leverage their new business celebrity status into franchises in all 50 states, with manufacturing in the Commonwealth of Puerto Rico. All of which would be done on the taxpayers' dime.

They immediately joined the International Franchise Association in Washington, D.C., which would provide them boiler plate language for franchising and a network of lobbyist to secure economic incentives in each state. Each jurisdiction would be vying for a Swampland as a result of all the media buzz about the company, and as a result the incentive packages would be chock-full of goodies. Grants, tax credits, no interest loans, buildings, infrastructure and job training would all be in the packages doled out by the states. This was easier than shooting ducks at the arcade. Swampland applicants would pay a franchise fee to corporate — i.e., Armando, Rosa, Sean and Paddy and with a mere pittance of an investment thanks to the largesse of state government, they would become full participants in the American free enterprise system.

While all this cash was pouring in, our four new millionaire entrepreneurs made a strategic decision that Armando and Rose would close the Glenn Apothecary and move manufacturing to Puerto Rico, where the Commonwealth was willing to foot the bill for everything.

Puerto Rico was offering to retrofit the abandoned Sears store as the new international manufacturing hub of Swampland. They also offered the company new facility grants that would allow it to hire Armando and Rosa as consultants for 10 years, with a seven figure no-cut contract. Responsibility under the contract included advising Swampland on strategic new directions and proactive approaches utilizing best practices to address and identify any new paradigm shifts. In essence, a contract that meant they would never have to show up for work. All the Commonwealth of Puerto Rico wanted in return was a ribbon cutting.

The ceremony for the new manufacturing facility was being pitched as a momentous rebirth of the private sector in Puerto Rico. Although the building had no equipment or employees, dignitaries and the press would be provided a virtual tour of what the facility would look like with 1,000 employees operating humming and glistening new machinery. Pixar was hired to create this aspirational rendering with James Earl Jones doing the voice-over. A hemp rope for cutting was strung across the front doors and a banner proclaiming 'Swampland: Our Date With Destiny' was slapped over the original Sears signage.

Hundreds were assembled for the ribbon cutting along with a throng of media and a gaggle of politicians and hangers-on. Center stage was the governor of Puerto Rico soaking in the attention and taking credit for everything. Also basking in the limelight was the Speaker of the House, President of the Senate, Director of the Economic Development Commission, President of the Puerto Rico Chamber of Commerce, President of the Amalgamated Brotherhood of Drug Laborers representing unions and the Executive Director of the Coalition for Free Enterprise who doubled as the governor's bag man in election years.

The event went off without a hitch. Beautiful weather, Ricky Martin singing "Born in Puerto Rico" over the loudspeakers, and two hours of meaningless self-congratulatory speeches followed by an hour of press availability when the same fatuous statements were repeated ad nauseam. As a political production, it was a smashing success.

While all this was going on in Puerto Rico, Sean and Paddy made plans to close the museum in Glenn and reposition the headquarters in Chicago. After consulting with Elaine Cabot Swarthmore, the threesome determined that employees in the new economy were simply a drag on the bottom line. They then reincorporated Swampland as a subsidiary of the National Political Corruption Hall of Fame making it eligible to be reincentivized for establishing a corporate headquarters in a WeWork facility in the Southside of Chicago. This location in a marginally disadvantaged zone of the city, made the new entity eligible for small business minority set-aside programs and tax free status for 13 years. It was all smoke and mirrors, but par for the course in the exciting world of economic development. Once established in WeWork and a mail drop created at the UPS Store, the mayor's office, in conjunction with the governor and the Illinois Chamber of Commerce, issued a lengthy press alert announcing their success in luring a new corporate headquarters from Michigan. Declaring the move of Swampland to Illinois as a testament to the robust business climate in the state and recognition that there is no better home for a business focused on political corruption than Chicago in the great state of Illinois.

As Sean and Paddy repositioned Swampland to continue to milk the government coffers, Berdenna and Senator Jaap Van Valkenberg were putting their $3.3 million piece of pork to good use. Rebranding Chesty Treasures Stimulating Beanery into Twin Peaks Rest Emporium would require an entirely new motif. This, of course, would require a consultant to create the new look, and they decided to go with West Michigan Strategies to the tune of $900,000. Coincidently, West Michigan Strategies just so happened to be the newly created consulting company of former Senator Jaap Van Valkenberg.

The former senator immediately went to work on the project by doing extensive research involving numerous visits to Hooters, The Tilted Kilt, Boobybungalow and Lil Darlings Strip Clubs. All this time and effort paid off when he came up with an eye-catching logo with two steep mountain peaks covered in a woman's bra with a steaming cup of coffee perched in the crevice. He knew he was onto something when his first billboard caused a multi-car collision on the nearby interstate.

Next stop for Twin Peaks was to secure designation of the derelict Toys "R" Us facility from which they would operate as a "Relic of Cultural Change" under the Historical Preservation Act. By doing so, they were able to obtain a $750,000 grant to maintain and restore the building to a contemporary equivalent of what it had been, which as a practical matter meant they could do anything they wanted.

While trying to be sensitive to local norms, Berdenna had erected on the roof two Eiffel Tower-type structures and instead of a bra connecting the two simply strung a banner with the inducement "Come Get It Hot." She also had posted a sign that truckers were welcome and that discrete parking was available in the back. She then had the staff of the former Tokyo Massage Parlor outfitted in western garb, which included cowboy hats, halter tops with fringe, see-through miniskirts and knee high boots with spurs. Each 'cowgirl' was instructed to welcome each customer with the greeting, "Are you ready to ride?" Background music alternated between the country hit 'I will marry you tomorrow, but let's honeymoon tonight' and in a nod to sophistication Nancy Sinatra singing, "These Boots Are Made for Walking."

The grand opening was a western production worthy of Hollywood. The Tokyo Massage ladies in their new theme attire formed a human funnel through which Berdenna in her own western outfit rode through on a horse twirling a lasso. Standing at the front door was the chairman of the Michigan Tourism Council standing between two cigar store Indians. When she reached the chairman, she threw the lasso around his neck and dragged him into the shop as the first customer while hundreds of would-be customers in S&M gear whooped and cheered. Traffic on the interstate was backed up for miles, with hundreds of semis waiting to avail themselves of some hot coffee and much needed rest. The new Toys "R" Us location was such a huge success that they decided to close the original location in Glenn.

FORTY-ONE

B ogey and Skeeter were enjoying their new-found success and celebrity status as co-hosts of the top-rated TV show *America's Most Wanted*. Critter Control and Smith & Wesson were putting huge dollars behind marketing the program, identifying the Georgia duo as the go-to guys on potential terrorism or just about anything the American public feared. Just the other day, they appeared on Tucker Carlson's show to corroborate foreign involvement in the Glenn attack after a "made in China" label was spotted in the shirt of the once-accused lead attacker Matilda Hoffenmeister. Now with her reappearance in Racine, the ratings of *America's Most Wanted* spiked to the point where it was challenging *Jeopardy* as the most trusted source for credible information on current events for Americans. Tucker, Bogey and Skeeter cited the idea that Matilda was a terrorist as more fake news by the liberal media.

The popularity of the show was not lost on Norma Jean Buckley, the former Waffle House waitress was now

CEO of Ravenous Redneck, a chain spinoff of diners modeled after Waffle Houses, now in expansion mode. As silent investors in Ravenous Redneck, Bogey and Skeeter had successfully promoted the chain on their TV show as the place where true Americans go to eat, and each time they did there was an appreciable bump in sales. Their endorsement, coupled with the patriotic fervor surrounding the chain opened a spigot of government cash to create new franchises around the country. Citizens began asking their legislators why their locale did not have a Ravenous Redneck. The demand was such that practically any entrepreneur qualified for a government incentive package to start a new Ravenous Redneck diner. The chain quickly became the primary expansion target of the Indian American Motel Owner's Association. A sure-fire indication that there would soon be one on every corner.

Concurrently, Norma Jean was becoming the Paula Deen of restaurants with her ever-present colloquial TV ads appearing on *Wrestling, Ultimate Fight Championship,* the *Home Shopping Network* and reruns of the *Andy Griffith Show*. Her homespun pitch that she was "fixin'" a "heart attack on a plate" with some sweet tea in a mason jar endeared her to millions. She would explain that "life is short, so eat dessert first," and then in a clarion call to all women simply state, "Quit being ugly, Southern cookin' makes you good lookin'."

The explosive growth of Ravenous Redneck and its phenomenal financial success was life changing for

Bogey, Skeeter and Norma Jean. After selling the enterprise to a Brazilian hedge fund for $150 million, they sought solitude with their newfound riches. Bogey built an identical replica of Graceland, Elvis Presley's home, in Hahira with a portrait of Elvis on velvet covering the living room wall. Here he would spend most of his days listening to George Strait and watching the fishing channel. Skeeter likewise built himself a mansion in Hahira, but his was modeled after the home of the late Dale Earnhardt and included a GoKart track adorned with ads for Bud Light, Red Man Chewing Tobacco and Midas Mufflers. He spent most days rounding the track in his miniature stock car while the NASCAR theme song *Runnin' Down a Dream* by Tom Petty blared over loudspeakers.

Norma Jean, on the other hand, decided to create a new aura for herself by adopting an entirely new lifestyle as if she was "to the manor born." She moved to Sweet Briar, Virginia, into a restored plantation home where she insisted on being called Miss Norma Jean and became active in the local chapter of the Daughters of the Confederacy. After making a $1 million gift to the local Sweet Briar College to further the preservation of Southern Womanhood, she was awarded an honorary Ph.D. in gender studies.

Sadly, after Bogey, Skeeter and Norma Jean cashed in with the $150 million, they abandoned *America's Most Wanted,* and she discontinued her promotional activity for Ravenous Redneck. In addition, the ownership by the

Brazilian group became a cause célèbre of Ann Coulter as another example of a foreign takeover of America resulting in the entire financial collapse of Ravenous Redneck and every franchise defaulting on obligations of their economic incentive packages. Most states explained the loss as just another example of unfair world trade practices and another reason to build a wall to stop illegal immigration.

Meanwhile the Texas contingent of Boone Cartwright, Brooke Blackstone, Montavious Sharp and Ron White were carving out new lives.

Boone's personal attorney Sumnter "Backroom" Pendergrass had successfully managed to have Boone spared from being indicted for tax evasion. The hiring of Bucky Thigpen, the son of U.S. Vice President Horatio Thigpen, as executive director of the Enron Ethics in Business Institute at Southern Methodist University had not gone unnoticed by the Department of Justice and the Internal Revenue Service. Coincidentally, about this same time, Boone decided to make a $1 million contribution to the Committee to Re-elect the President as a token of support for his administration's ongoing efforts to protect and defend the free enterprise system. Unrelated, but shortly thereafter, the Criminal Division of the Department of Justice announced that further investigation of ERR LLC and its principals was being discontinued as a matter of prosecutorial discretion in the furtherance of justice.

After successfully dodging prosecution, Boone left the Dallas area and moved to the Cayman Islands where he bought a house previously owned by the Madoff Trust and took up residence with his confidential assistant Debbie Darling. The two of them announced that they were dedicated to running the Enron Institute from the Caymans where business could be conducted in a transparent fashion without excessive government interference.

Brooke Blackstone successfully combined her separation payout from ERR LLC with a grant from the Progress Woman's Economic Development Fund of Texas to establish the "Let Them Eat Cake" personal shopping company. Her relationship with Boone soured after she was caught in flagrante delicto with the company pilot and photos of the two of them in compromising positions were spread over the front page of the Texas edition of the National Enquirer. This exposure, however, was a boon for her business, as women's rights groups took up her cause as an example of the double standard imposed on female executives in the oil industry. The Dallas chapter of the Association of Oil Wives honored her as 'Working Girl of the Year' and designated her company as a preferred vendor for all the members' shopping needs. Let Them Eat Cake became a national role model for young female entrepreneurs.

Under the leadership of Montavious Sharp, The America First Foundation (AFF) in Oil City, Pennsylvania flourished. Strategically located on the East coast of the

U.S. near the liberal effete bastions of Boston, New York City, Philadelphia and Washington, D.C., the foundation was able to milk those donor bases while maintaining an aura of middle America. The America First slogan, "You Are on Your Own" endeared it to the right wing and even won recognition and plaudits on the Laura Ingraham show as an inspiration for all freedom loving Americans. At the same time, Montavious was able to shame liberals into support by carefully crafting a pitch and a message laying blame on almost every ire of society on the inherent injustices of class structure in America. He was so effective that the Reverend Al Sharpton, through his National Action Network, awarded Montavious the Master of Obfuscation in Fundraising Award.

Montavious was a darling of the media. The so called headquarters in Oil City was simply a P.O. Box in a UPS store. He actually lived in a brownstone on 5th Avenue in New York City, owned by the foundation, which according to the AFF website allowed him to promote American ideas in a diverse environment absent class subjugation and devoid of bourgeois restraints. No one even really understood what the foundation accomplished, but it was widely regarded as extremely successful.

Sadly, Ron White did not fare as well as his other three compatriots from ERR LLC. His concept for a combined coin laundry along with a bar/restaurant under the trademarked name "Suds" proved unsuccessful. His first attempt at the venture in an abandoned J.C. Penny store never got off the ground. For some reason, many of the patrons found the smell of bleach in the restaurant unacceptable. In addition, the washing machines on the balcony overlooking the restaurant would periodically overflow flooding the customers below with muddled gray dirty detergent water, creating what the health department called an "unparalleled toxic eating environment." If this wasn't enough, despite being director of real estate for ERR, LLC, he had failed to thoroughly examine the title of the former J.C. Penny store, which as it turns out had been built on a former Level 1 Superfund Site which still emanated methane gas.

Ron quickly exhausted his ERR, LLC separation monies and was forced to declare bankruptcy. He moved in with his mother and became modestly successful selling cemetery plots with the catchy slogan, "Real Estate You Keep Forever."

FORTY-TWO

Governor Willard "Little Wiley" Buckley of Arizona sat in his expansive office in the Capitol ruminating on how to capitalize on his last year in office. It was then out of the corner of his eye, he caught the Fox News coverage of what they termed was a movement behind the Wave of the Future Church and its aerial spraying antiterrorist activity. Glenn Beck was calling Ingrid an archangel in the fight against foreign enemies and declaring the Wave of the Future Church as a citadel of God fearing patriots. What was of special interest to the governor, however, was the number of faithful willing to show up each day and plop down $10 to participate in the twice a day aerial holy water missions.

Before entering politics, "Little Wiley" Buckley had made a fortune in the used car business. He called the business Buckley's Car Storage leading people to believe that the cars had been in storage and hence the pristine condition and low mileage. In fact, none had been in storage, but actually rebuilt after being deemed totaled for insurance purposes and the low mileage a result of simply rolling back the odometer. His entry into politics was precipitated by an action by the Arizona Department of Consumer Protection to close down his business as a "criminally corrupt enterprise" defrauding the people of Arizona on an ongoing basis. Little Wiley used this adverse publicity to catapult himself from obscurity to the governor's office by claiming to be just another small businessman trying to survive under the boot heels of government oppression. He cleverly made his motto "Make Arizona Great Again" and successfully recycled thousands of Trump 2020 MAGA hats to give away as he barnstormed the state with a series of "Nothing is Free in Life" rallies. He won in a landslide.

Although Little Wiley portrayed himself as a self-made small businessman, he actually had inherited considerable wealth from his father, "Big Wiley." It turns out, Big Wiley had made millions by scamming the indigenous Mohave Indian tribe into selling him "worthless" land, which he knew but they did not, it was where the government planned to build a damn to create Lake Havasu. Big Wiley then sold the land to the government at a premium and kept what would be the shoreline for development into resort property. Later he would convince the Arizona Department of Economic Development to fund the relocation of London Bridge 5,400 miles from the Thames to Lake Havasu in the Arizona desert as a tourism revitalization project. What London Bridge had to do with Lake Havasu was never completely understood, but was clearly a testament to the sales ability of Big Wiley Buckley. The family had a streak of DNA straight from P.T. Barnum.

Watching the burgeoning popularity of the Wave of the Future Church and the crowds it drew to Glenn made Governor Little Wiley Buckley excited at the thought of recruiting the entire church to Lake Havasu as a means of revitalizing the tired family holdings. It would also be a way to give his 22-year-old ne'er-do-well son "Junior Wiley" something to do and possibly a sinecure for life. He immediately called the obsequious director of the Department of Commerce he had appointed and ordered him to prepare a comprehensive relocation incentive package for the Wave of the Future Church to move to Lake Havasu. The package was to include free land and buildings, tax exempt status, job creation stipends, cash grants and a runway with viewing stands to accommodate the twice daily flights and seating for patrons who made $10 donations to the church. The flights would be billed as Angel Flights commemorating the defense of London and its famous bridge going back to the days of Winston Churchill and WWII. Although as a religious based institution, it would be a nonprofit, the proposal did call for a management authority with three compensated board members — Bishop Ingrid Johansen, Red Johansen and "Junior Wiley" Buckley.

Red Johansen couldn't believe what he was hearing when the call came in from the Arizona Department of Commerce. In all his years in Economic Development, he had never heard or seen such a sweet offer. No cash up front and a total turnkey operation. Income for life for he and Ingrid and even a company plane available at their beck and call when not in use for the twice daily official church function. He had no idea who Junior Wiley Buckley was, but who cared. This was as good as it got, but he decided why not one more ask. How about a company car? Done. He and Ingrid were moving to Arizona.

Two weeks later, Governor William "Little Wiley" Buckley of Arizona issued a press release announcing a major economic development coup for the state. He was proud to announce that the Wave of the Future Church in Glenn, Michigan was relocating to Lake Havasu. The governor cited the administration's support for religious liberty and the respect the God fearing citizens of Arizona had for the sanctity of the separation of church and state as the major inducements for the move. No mention was made of the financial package other than a footnote that monetary details will be worked out by the Department of Commerce and a three-member panel of directors of the church.

FORTY-THREE

G overnor Earl Baumgarten was airlifted from the docks to Racine Memorial Hospital where a team of doctors used an improvised bilge pump to resuscitate the governor. His presence in the facility created a frenzy of activity, including an overnight candlelight vigil by the local chapter of the Sierra Club and a contingent of stalwarts from the Save the Whale Movement.

The President of the United States, prior to announcing his plan to defund the Environmental Protection Agency (EPA), tweeted that the governor's heroics reminded him of General Patton in time of war who advised:

"The time to take counsel of your fears is before you make an important battle decision. That's the time to listen to every fear you can imagine. When you have collected all the facts and fears and made your decision, turn off all your fears and go ahead."

The prime minister of Canada called on the Parliament to award the governor its highest commendation the 'Order of Canada' in recognition of his selfless act to protect the country from an onslaught of marauding fish. Tributes poured in from religious leaders, civic organizations, environmental groups and even Dunkin Donuts who proclaimed how the governor had proven how "Making a dip can make a difference."

As the acting Governor of Michigan, Lieutenant Governor Theodious Adamowski watched this unfold in neighboring Wisconsin, he knew it was time to implement the plan agreed upon by him, Governor Baumgarten and Attorney General Stanford Dodge. He immediately issued a press release proclaiming how humbled he was to now be acting governor and that if Governor Baumgarten should decide to remain in Wisconsin, he would proceed on behalf of the people of Michigan in a "transparent" fashion with their best interest at heart and devoid of any of the self-dealing too often the case in Lansing. Once the release hit the wires, he called Attorney General Dodge to let him know the "Sanford Plan" was in motion and then by executive order created a "constitutional revision commission" with him as chairman at a six figure salary, plus benefits, paving his way for departure from state government and his well-deserved pension. Meanwhile, the attorney general who was next in line for governor, called the Governor of Wisconsin to assure him that he would look most fondly on that governor's run for chairman of the National Governor's Association if he would create a suitable position for Governor Baumgarten and his paramour Miss Hoffenmeister, so that they stayed in Wisconsin. All of which made perfect sense to the governor of the dairy state who in turn announced that he was creating a commission on the preservation of the Great Lakes and that former Governor of Michigan, Earl Baumgarten, had agreed to become chairman and that Matilda Hoffenmeister would serve as executive director both to be compensated in a manner appropriate to the positions.

As the machinations were underway to transfer power to the attorney general, while making the former governor and lieutenant governor financially secure, Clive Barnsley was being touted in the media as some sort of modern day Admiral Nimitz. Fox News described his trip as a "Daring night time attack on would be invaders of the USA" and CNN cited it as a "historic moment in protecting our environment and preventing climate change." His stature in Wisconsin was such that he was asked to serve as grand marshal of the Great Wisconsin Cheese Festival Parade in Little Chute, Wisconsin. A much coveted honor which catapulted him into the position of President of the Wisconsin Cheese Makers Association, a taxpayer funded body, where he would be compensated for doing little if anything.

When Attorney General Dodge assumed the governorship he feigned surprise at his good fortune and declared that it was with "great humility" that he accepted the office of governor and that in the interest of moving

forward and "not dwelling on the past," he was discontin-
uing all and any public corruption investigations so that the
state would look forward to a "brighter future."

EPILOGUE

Two Years Later

The pipe still protrudes out of the ground on the old golf course, but the black goo dripping into the Jiffy Lube recycling canister had long run dry. There are a few other remnants of the incentivized Glenn days. Ten yards off shore in Lake Michigan, beach goers are always befuddled by a battered sign that for some reason, simply says in Spanish, *"Que tengas un feliz dia en la playa."* Another sign on the road by the old clubhouse, after being pummeled over a couple years by so many shotgun blasts that all that is readable is, *"This far you may come and no farther."* A statement that feeds local lore that this site had once been a secret operations center in the war on terror.

The coffee shop, apothecary, ERR LLC, Wave of the Future Church and the National Political Corruption Hall of Fame no longer call Glenn home and the promised jobs have all been a mirage. Lives and livelihoods have moved on. Keith and Kevin Jackson aviation sightseeing operations is now defunct and the two of them have become co-chairs of the local chapter of QAnon blaming a "deep state cabal" and "satanic forces" for the demise of their business. Dr. Mandalay Violin returned to Haiti for a brief visit where she was received as a conquering hero for her medical accomplishments with the under served in the United States. Her fame is such that she was appointed national director of public health for all of Haiti which she directs remotely from Miami Beach.

Clive Barnsley, Matilda Hoffenmeister and her lover, Governor Earl Baumgarten all are thriving in Wisconsin. Clive received the highest recognition possible when he was titled Cheesehead of the Year by the Wisconsin Cheese Maker Association which he just so happens to run. Earl and Matilda have taken on an entirely new persona. In recognition of their daring exploits to save the environment, they were appointed by the Governor of Wisconsin to well-paying positions with the Commission for the Preservation of the Great Lakes with responsibilities that include wearing Birkenstocks and flannel shirts on a daily basis.

Dreams do come true and they did for Jack Hightower and Audrey Richenberg. After successfully making the auto-train, Audrey, aka Marilyn, fulfilled her commitment by staging a show in the bar car as a sultry Marilyn singing Chattanooga Choo, while mounting a broomstick horse intended as a gift for a grandchild of one of the passengers. The bar car became so raucous that the defibrillator had to be used on three different elderly gentlemen who had collapsed. Upon arrival at The Villages they were met by Jack's old friend Merwyn Schlotsky who had arranged for Hollywood spotlights to sweep the sky and presented them with their very own golf cart emblazoned with "Tired Blood. Take Geritol". Audrey's act was warmly received with two a day Tuesday through Saturday one at 3:30 pm and the late show at 5:30. Their rent free condo overlooked Interstate 75, but since they were both deaf as bats it was quite acceptable and Jack relished the fact he was recognized as a regular with his daily visit to Cracker Barrel. As far as they were concerned, it just didn't get any better.

Rosa and Armando are flourishing in Puerto Rico, where both have become prominent members of the San Juan Chamber of Commerce and single digit handicappers in golf. They are held in such esteem that they have been asked by the Puerto Rico Manufacturers Association to co-chair the Drugs Don't Work Program to prevent drugs in the workplace.

Boone Cartwright, Brooke Blackstone, Montavious Sharp and Ron White transitioned in different directions. Boone and his confidential assistant Debbie Darling have taken up permanent residence in the Cayman Islands out of reach of the long arm of the law and where bank accounts are inaccessible by the authorities. Brooke's "Let Them Eat Cake" personal shopping business is burgeoning as oil prices have doubled and the oil wives' rights movement have swelled creating the proverbial perfect storm in high end merchandising. Montavious is a cause célèbre in New York City and, for the matter, around the country, known for his vociferous advocacy on behalf of capitalism and the free market. He is the darling of Fox News and *The Wall Street Journal*, where he touts his humble upbringing as proof anyone in America can make it if we only get government off the backs of people. Ron, meanwhile, continues to sell cemetery plots and actually is doing quite well after he began to appear in ads on the local cable channel explaining how you could fund your plot with a reverse mortgage.

Bogey Jackson, Skeeter Williams and Norma Jean Buckley lived out their lives in relatively wealthy obscurity. *America's Most Wanted* TV show ran its course and was replaced by reruns of *Gunsmoke*. Bogey and Skeeter still reside in Hahira dabbling in their hobbies of collecting Elvis memorabilia and playing stock car driver. Each year in recognition of their local fame, they have been asked to judge the Miss Teenage Hahira Beauty Pageant. Norma Jean, after cashing out with Ravenous Redneck, is the Grand Dame of the Sweetbriar Social Swirl.

Jaap and Berdenna VanValkenberg eventually sold the Twin Peaks Rest Emporium for a sizable profit to the Teamster's Pension Fund, looking for a place to convert their proceeds from Las Vegas investments. Jaap and Berdenna have used the cash to buy an event center in Lansing called The Watering Hole near the Capitol, which can be rented to lobbyists and used for fundraisers for political campaigns. It turned out to be quite successful after it became the only spot to provide free "to go" bags for all elected officials attending a function.

Swampland was designated the Franchise of the Year Award by the National Franchise Association. Elaine Cabot Swarthmore, with the unlimited financial backing of the Goldman Sachs Philanthropic Fund, became the female equivalent of Jack Welch as a management guru. Sean O'Malley and Paddy Fitzpatrick maintain a lucrative consulting role with the company providing advice and counsel involving foosball and related activities. In this capacity, they assumed the title of ambassadors of good-will, which requires them to play mindless hours of foosball at select Swampland locations.

Finally, Red and Ingrid Johansson live out their days operating Wave of the Future Church in Lake Havasu, Arizona. The church acquired national prominence after aligning itself with Liberty University and persuading Jerry Falwell, the past president of Liberty to become an expert in residence where he proselytizes on the importance of media management by faith-based institutions. This program won national acclaim and occupies most of Ingrid's attention. Red, on the other hand, spends most of his time cruising the desert highways of Arizona with the top down in his new red Corvette convertible.

CPSIA information can be obtained
at www.ICGtesting.com
Printed in the USA
LVHW051929080321
680888LV00012B/1702